CHRIS MULDOON

CHRIS MULDOON

by

Rita Shields

Illustrated by Ray Abel

DAVID McKAY COMPANY, INC.
New York
1965

CHRIS MULDOON

COPYRIGHT © 1965 BY
Rita Shields

LIBRARY OF CONGRESS CATALOG CARD NUMBER: 65-14921
MANUFACTURED IN THE UNITED STATES OF AMERICA

For
ALL MY BOYS
those whom I have taught
those whom I am teaching
those whom I hope to teach

1: *Positive and Negative*

Chris was twelve, and his interests ranged from A to Z. His grin was quick, as quick as a flash of sunlight upon a mirror, and just as bright. His teacher knew that grin and watched for it as carefully as she watched the thermostat for any change in classroom temperature.

"That Chris Muldoon," the neighbors said. But Mom knew the real Chris, the sweetness and the strength of him under all the nonsense, and wheedling and banter.

His room was a combination junior museum, frontier trading post, and advance headquarters for the flight to the moon.

"Mom darling, just let me stay up one more little old hour; I have to finish this experiment," was almost a nightly ritual.

But gentle Mom had the final say, and when Chris knew that his coaxing and wheedling had been stretched to the very end, he gave a quick peck to her cheek, and with a "Night, Mom" was off to bed, but not always to sleep.

There were many things on the mind of Chris

Muldoon. Though his over-all and greatest interest was outer space, right now he was preoccupied with the scientific principles of positive and negative as it applied to his own life. It seemed almost impossible for anything plus to happen to him without having a minus to pull it down.

For instance, right here in this room. He could lie in the upper bunk of his bed (and what wheedling it had taken to get Mom to buy bunk beds for just one boy) and see clear to the ocean just four San Francisco blocks away. He could notice every change in the sky, and many times he had jumped from bed crying, "I know it's a flying saucer."

But he couldn't look out the window without seeing old Mr. Kitchenger's house. Old Mr. Kitchenger apparently disliked all children, but most of all he seemed to dislike Chris Muldoon. "Hum," he was always growling, "it's a man's hand he needs." Now since Dad had returned to the Veterans' hospital, Mr. Kitchenger seemed to be meaner than ever.

Chris would like to shut Mr. Kitchenger's house from his view forever, but there it was. He couldn't be a sky watcher without having Kitchenger's house in sight.

Then there were Percy and the lab.

The city schools had a laboratory program where specially selected pupils went twice a week for ad-

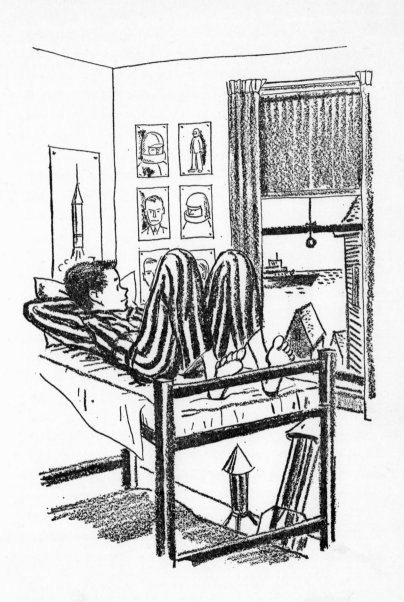

vanced science lessons. Only one child from each High 6th grade of every school in the city was selected. Chris was chosen from his High 6th. His mother was jubilant, and immediately phoned the hospital, and left a message for Dad. As she sat at dinner with Chris, the bell rang and there was a congratulatory telegram from Dad.

"Oh, Chris, I know you'll make us proud of you."

"I'll try, Mom."

Chris was more eager to go to the lab than he had been about anything else. But who should have been selected from the other High 6th in Westcliff School? Percy.

Percy!

Ever since Kindergarten, Percy had been in Chris' hair, according to Chris' expressive speech. Literally, though, nothing much more than the fine teeth of a small comb could get into his closely cropped reddish-brown hair.

M.T., Laurie, Percy and Chris had gone to school together since Kindergarten. M.T. was the nearest thing Chris had to a brother; almost a twin, in fact. Chris was only one week younger than M.T.

Laurie. Well, for a girl Laurie was wonderful. After school she wore jeans, kicked off her shoes, raced along the water's edge with Chris and M.T., gave splash for splash, but took them, too.

The three of them had spent all their school days avoiding Percy who wore big dark-rimmed glasses, and from the very first grade seemed to know everything and was never reluctant about letting it be known.

Now there was the positive and negative again for Chris. He couldn't go to the wonderful, special lab without having Percy there, too.

Chris stopped his musings and jumped from bed. He thought he had seen a flash. One could never tell what might be in the skies these nights. In an instant he was at the window, and then he let out a low, disgusted groan.

It was only Mr. Kitchenger going around with his flashlight, making sure his house was safe without and within.

Chris returned to bed more awake than ever and continued his line of thought: positive, negative; plus, minus; super, awful. They all seemed to go together, at least for Chris.

Take the astronauts, for instance. No one was more wildly interested than Chris. From our first break-through into space, he followed every orbital flight. He read every word about them, and was fairly glued to the TV every minute of the flights.

When the United States spacecraft, Ranger 7,

successfully hit the moon, Chris danced wildly around the living room as an excited commentator said, "We should land men on the moon in four years."

"You bet!" Chris shouted. Then he drew up short. Four years. He was twelve now. That would make him only sixteen. He had hoped to be the first man on the moon.

Remembering now, his quick grin flashed, and he squirmed to get more comfortable in bed. Oh well, let somebody else be the first, but he'd get to the moon some day for sure. And without Percy, he hoped.

He did get rid of Percy for a while, but there was a negative, a great big negative to that.

When school opened for the spring term, for the first time in the history of Westcliff School there was a man teacher. As the children were in the yard waiting for the bell, everyone was hoping to be in the man's class. As they filed into their rooms, to the great joy of Chris, M.T., and Laurie, there he was in their classroom—Room 1.

As the morning progressed, their admiration for Mr. Lawrence increased. Super. Boy, he was really super. They were so happy, they didn't even bother about Percy.

Just before noon, the principal, Mrs. Johnstone,

7

came into the room. The class, she said, was too crowded, so ten children were to be put into the High 6th in Room 2.

"Will the following children please come forward?" she asked as she started reading names from the list.

Chris held his breath, hoping that his name would not be called.

Percy's name was number eight. Chris held his feelings in check. He could still be called. So could M.T. or Laurie.

Mrs. Johnstone called numbers nine and ten. Chris had all he could do to keep from shouting out his glee. He, Laurie, and M.T. would be together. They would have Mr. Lawrence, and Percy would be gone. What a wonderful start for their last term at Westcliff School.

Chris' quick grin lit up his green eyes, and he crossed glances first with M.T. and then with Laurie. After all these years they were rid of Percy.

He was so intent on sharing his happiness with Laurie and M.T. he didn't realize what was going on at the front of the room.

The ten had lined up and at Mrs. Johnstone's nod started from the room.

"Now the rest of you sit quietly until Miss Foster comes in."

"Miss Foster!" Chris was so shocked, he shouted out before he even realized it.

"Yes," Mrs. Johnstone said, "Miss Foster will teach in Room 1. Mr. Lawrence will have Room 2, and, Chris Muldoon, I'll see you in my office after school."

After school was the least of Chris' worries as he sadly watched Mr. Lawrence and the chosen ten leave Room 1.

So he had gotten rid of Percy, but to do it he had to lose Mr. Lawrence, and have Miss Foster for another term.

Then, of course, he wasn't completely rid of Percy. There he was twice a week at the lab. And next to Percy's showing off his superior scientific knowledge, he seemed to get particular satisfaction out of telling Chris all about the wonders of Mr. Lawrence and the happy time in Room 2.

"Positive and negative," Chris murmured sleepily and burrowed down in the covers. But before sleep finally came, the last negative pricked at his mind.

Yesterday they had made plans for their class play. Miss Foster announced that it would be a Columbus play.

Chris put his hand over his mouth to keep from groaning out loud. He could feel the dejection of everyone around.

9

"It seems so right to have a Columbus play. You children live at the sea just as he did. He played on the shores of Genoa. You . . ."

Chris didn't listen. He knew exactly what she was going to say. This was the third term the class had Miss Foster. This was their third play about Columbus. Miss Foster always announced a Columbus play with the speech about children playing at the sea.

Chris knew he would have to resign himself to the play, as the rest of the class did. But just this afternoon at the lab, Percy told him about the program that Room 2 was going to give. It was to have a space theme, and he, Percy, was to do a science experiment right on the stage.

Chris could feel his eyes getting heavy with sleep, so he made a last effort to put his thoughts on something positive. He didn't want to dream of Percy, or of Columbus, either.

Maybe if he concentrated enough, he might dream of an astronaut.

"Maybe all the astronauts," he murmured drowsily.

2: *Rope Ladder*

Chris dreamed neither of ancient explorers nor modern astronauts. After a restful, dreamless sleep, he met his mother at the breakfast table, his eyes shining, his quick grin flashing, all ready for the adventures of a new day.

"Now, Chris," she admonished at the end of the meal, "remember that Miss Foster has thirty-six boys and girls in the class. Try not to make her day too hard."

"I'll try, Mom. But gee—Columbus!"

"What's wrong with Columbus?"

"Nothing, Mom, but gee, this will be our third play about him."

"That's perfectly all right. I'm sure Miss Foster knows what she's doing. When you're the teacher, you can decide what type of play to give."

"When I'm the teacher?" Chris fell back into the chair he had just vacated. "Jeepers, Mom. I'm not going to be a teacher. I'm going to be an astronaut. I'm going to the moon."

"Well, you're going to school right now. So start your countdown."

Chris gave a quick kiss to the back of her neck. " 'Bye, Mom," he said as he bolted to the door.

"Chris!" she called, "You forgot your lunch."

In two leaps he was back across the kitchen reaching for his lunch box. "Thanks for reminding me, Mom."

"Really, Chris, you are so forgetful. I'm sure it is just that you don't pay any attention. For one who has nothing on his mind to worry about.

"Nothing on my mind! Nothing to worry about!" Chris reeled back in astonishment.

Mom laughed and gave him a quick shove with a gentle hand. "I know. On your way, astronaut."

Chris met M.T. at the corner, and the two of them met Laurie at the next corner. They crossed the street just in time to avoid Percy.

"Let me tell you what Percy told me yesterday," Chris said, and went on to give an account of Room 2's proposed space program, and Percy's part in it.

"Wouldn't you know?" Laurie said.

"And we're stuck with Columbus," M.T. said dejectedly. "Miss Foster will start testing for parts today. Its our turn for the auditorium."

"Might as well be today as any day. It's just as bad whenever it starts." With an air of resignation, Chris kicked a pebble out of the way.

But they didn't start as expected.

As Miss Foster wrote the plan of the day's work on the board, she said, "Boys and girls, I'm sorry. We won't be able to get our parts for the play today. There's to be a special assembly."

Chris sought M.T.'s eyes and mouthed the word, "Reprieve."

Chris was prepared to like anything that happened at the assembly, so relieved was he to put the detested one back a while. But he wasn't in the auditorium long until he sat straight and intent out of pure interest. The theme of the assembly was fire prevention, and one of the city firemen was explaining carefully and dramatically all the fire hazards that exist in the home, and how each child could make himself a committee of one to see that his home was free of such hazards, and how he could be prepared in case of fire.

Chris was fascinated as the fireman displayed a rope ladder, showed how to make one, and advocated that every child have one in his room in case his normal escape route would be cut off.

Chris was so eager to get home and make a rope ladder that he found it difficult getting through the rest of the day. Miss Foster called for his attention no less than six times.

After school he found it hard refusing M.T. and

Laurie when they urged him to go to the beach with them and play in the caves.

He dashed home, changed his clothes, took time only to drink a glass of milk before he went to the basement. He worked carefully and steadily and had the rope ladder finished and in his room just as his mother called him for dinner.

Now to test it. He was preoccupied all during dinner, and afterward could hardly wait for bedtime. As soon as reasonable, he said good night to Mom and started to his room.

She called him back and put her hand to his forehead. "Chris, are you all right?"

"Yeh, Mom. Why?"

"Why? It's only eight-thirty and you're going to bed."

"I'm okay, Mom. 'Night."

He put on his pajamas and lay in bed for a while. Then quietly he lowered himself to the floor, tiptoed to the window and looked out. Good. Kitchenger's house was lighted. He would be guided by the lights.

Carefully and slowly he raised the window, trying not to make any noise. He anchored the rope ladder as the fireman advised, lowered it out the window, and started his descent. The rope was rough and cutting on his bare feet. The chill night air beat against his pajamaed figure and gave him an exhilarated feeling. One step and then another and his feet touched the firm cold ground. He had made it! His ladder was a success.

He stood there for a moment looking around, and then the elation drained from him. He had made it. So what? True, it would be wonderful in an emergency; it was good to know that it would work. But after all his excitement of the morning, his eagerness to start work on it, his enthusiasm while working, he felt somehow cheated by his tiny little trip out the window.

Then he grinned in the darkness. He just wouldn't be cheated. He'd have some fun on the ladder. He climbed back up, then down, then up. It was fun. He was getting used to the rope and his feet were smarting less and less. He was acquiring speed, too. Up, down, up, down. He forgot everything else around him.

Just as he touched the ground for about the twentieth time he heard Mr. Kitchenger shouting, "Prowler! Prowler!"

Next there were two loud reports and Chris crouched down, leaning against the house just as something whizzed by his head.

In a few minutes all was pandemonium. Lights went on all over the neighborhood. There was more shouting, and running, and flashlights, and then a police siren.

"There he is! There he is!" he heard. Rough hands pulled him to his feet.

"Officer O'Looney." Chris recognized the policeman who was holding him.

"Chris Muldoon," the policeman said, "what in the world are you up to now?"

Chris tried to explain about the assembly this morning, and about the rope ladder, but he had a hard time with all the confusion and Mr. Kitchenger shouting, "That Chris Muldoon. It's a man's hand he needs!"

Then his mother was there outside the window and amidst all the noise and confusion her soft voice was staccato clear. "Chris, go into the house this minute."

Chris started to open his mouth.

"In!" she commanded, pointing to the open window, "and take that ladder with you."

Chris scrambled up the ladder, and pulled it in after him.

"It's a man's hand he needs!" Mr. Kitchenger was still shouting.

"I agree with you, Mr. Kitchenger," Mom said.

Chris, crouching just inside the window, heard

Officer O'Looney trying to explain to her about the fireman and the rope ladder.

"Granted, Officer O'Looney, but there must have been hundreds at that assembly. Are they all climbing up and down on rope ladders? No. Just my Chris."

"Ah now, Mrs. Muldoon, maybe they haven't the imagination. You know Chris tells me he's going to the moon some day."

"Yes, I know. And there are times, Officer O'Looney, and this is one, when I would like to *send* him to the moon."

"Now, now, Mrs. Muldoon. Come, I'll escort you to your front door."

Chris could hear Mom coming down the hall, and her step was just as staccato as her voice had been.

Mmm. Those were bad signs. Chris wondered about her cheeks. Were there two round pink patches on her cheekbones? When she was very, very angry (and that wasn't often) you could always tell by her voice, her walk, and those two pink circles on her cheekbones.

"Chris, come out here," she called from the kitchen.

As he entered the room he looked at her cheeks. Yes. Pink, very, very pink.

She indicated the place opposite her at the table.

"Chris, what in the world is the matter with you?"

"Mom, I didn't mean anything."

"You never mean anything. But you've embarrassed me before the whole neighborhood."

"Mom, I'm sorry."

"You're always sorry . . . too late. You never think. All you want is adventure and excitement." She paused as if to gather strength, and then went on, "Do you know what *impulsive* means?"

"Yes, Mom."

"Well, that's what you are, impulsive and forgetful, and they go hand in hand, and are going to lead you into serious trouble if you aren't careful."

Her head went down on the table and through muffled sobs she said, "You could have been shot tonight."

"Oh, Mom, Mom." Chris was kneeling beside her, his arms around her. That was worse than anything to see Mom cry, and to know that he had caused it. He'd rather have any punishment.

"Mom, Mom, I'm sorry. Please stop crying. I'll do anything. Anything you say. Please, Mom."

Slowly her sobs stopped. She raised her head and looked straight at Chris. "All right, I'll take you at your word."

"Mom?"

"Just a minute. I'll explain," she said as she left

the kitchen and returned almost immediately carrying an envelope.

"This came the other day. It's a letter from Aunt Jane. Your cousin, Pamela, is getting married next month and they want you to be in the wedding party."

"What does that mean?"

"Penny is to be a junior bridesmaid, and you are to be her partner. You will escort her up the aisle."

Chris could hardly find his voice. "How will I have to dress?"

"Like every young usher in a wedding party. Black trousers with a satin stripe up the side."

"Satin?"

"Yes," Mom went on almost gleefully. "A white jacket."

"White jacket! Oh no, Mom."

She ignored him. "And a black bow tie."

"Bow tie!"

"And black pumps."

"Oh, Mom, please, please. Don't make me."

"Remember you promised, anything, anything."

"Oh but, Mom, this."

"At first I was going to try to get you out of it, but now I'm not. I think it will be good for you."

"But suppose someone sees me?"

"That's the idea."

"Mom, I think I like Mr. Kitchenger's idea better."

"Mr. Kitchenger's idea?"

"Yes. The man's hand. I don't think it would be nearly so bad."

Mom laughed, and just then Chris shivered from head to toe.

"Chris, Chris." She was at his side in a minute. "I'm afraid you've caught a cold."

Chris grinned. "No, Mom; it's just the thought of that wedding."

"Go get your robe and slippers anyhow. I think we each could do with a nice cup of hot chocolate."

3: *Blood Brothers*

Subdued, Chris sat opposite his mother at the breakfast table next morning. He was contrite about the incident of the rope ladder last night, but he was staggered by the thought of the wedding.

Suppose they saw him? What would Laurie think, and M.T., and Percy? But most of all M. T.

He thought about it all through breakfast, and went the long way to school to be sure he wouldn't meet M.T. before he had decided what to do.

He walked around the block twice, and it would soon be time for the bell to ring.

Yes, he would have to do it. That would be the best way. He would have to tell M.T.

The bell rang just as Chris reached the schoolyard. He saw M.T. entering the building and ran to catch up with him. He came alongside M.T. and cast a quick look down the hall. Miss Foster was on hall duty, and Mrs. Johnstone was standing outside her office door. Still he managed to convey to M.T. that he had something very serious to tell him.

"At first recess?"

"No. After school."

He could sense M.T.'s immediate interest. He knew that if there was anything that M.T. loved, it was a secret, or a mystery. His blond hair, cropped as short as Chris', his blue eyes, and freckled face came alive with the look of a sleuth on the trail.

At every recess, at lunch time, between lessons, he pressed for more details, but Chris was adamant. It had to be after school.

"In the caves?" M.T. asked out of the side of his mouth as he passed his desk.

"No. At your house or mine. I don't want Laurie to know."

Now he had really done it. Every time he looked up for the rest of the day he saw M.T. watching him. His curiosity was really aroused. Chris could tell that M.T. could hardly wait for dismissal. Chris dreaded the time to come. He hated the thought of what he had to tell.

The minute they were out of the school building M.T. put his arm around Chris' shoulder. "Your house," he said. "I want to see that rope ladder."

"All right," Chris answered. Well, maybe it would be just as well. He had been worrying all day how to tell his dreadful news. Maybe the rope ladder would be a good lead.

"Sharpo. But Sharpo!" M.T. said as he examined the ladder minutely.

Even in his misery a pleased flush spread over Chris' face. "Sharpo" was the height of M.T.'s praise.

In an instant M.T. was at the window, the rope ladder in his hand. "I want to try it."

"No. No!" Chris shouted excitedly.

"Why not? What's it for, anyhow?"

Then Chris told him about last night and the rope ladder.

M.T. sat on the floor with his back against the window. His eyes lighted with excitement at the story.

Chris found himself living up to the excitement. Unconsciously he got more and more dramatic. "And then a bullet whizzed by my head."

"Real live shooting? Honest to goodness, Chris?"

"Honest to goodness."

"Sharpo. Double sharpo."

Chris' heart gave a leap at the praise. Now there was no stopping him. The shouts of the neighbors, the sirens, himself in the hands of Officer O'Looney, he played them all to the hilt.

M.T. sat there speechless, his mouth wide open. Chris knew it was from admiration, so he carried on until he told of climbing back up the rope ladder and into his room.

"Sharpo, sharpo," was all that M.T. seemed to be able to say. Then he looked searchingly at Chris. "Say, were you fooling me all day? You said you had something terrible to tell me. That's the most super thing I've ever heard in a long time."

Chris was tempted to let it go at that. It wasn't often that he won such glowing praise from M.T. Still why had he brought him here in the first place? Because he had decided it would be better to tell him rather than take the chance of being seen in his wedding finery. It would be better to win M.T. to his side first.

"There's more to it," Chris said hesitantly.

"What?" M.T. was all eager excitement.

"The awful part."

"Well, go on. Go on."

Chris could see the sleuth in M.T. again.

"Then Mom came in."

"And?" M.T. pressed.

Chris was unable to go on.

"Did you get punished?"

Chris nodded mutely.

"So what?" M.T. asked. "What's a little old punishment after such a super experience as you had?"

"It wasn't a little punishment."

26

"It wasn't?" M.T. rose to his feet, his quarter inch of blond hair more bristling than ever. "Come on, Chris, give. Remember you invited me here to tell me. You've got to."

"No. I can still change my mind. I told you part."

"Yeh, but not the real serious part. You have to."

"No, I don't. There's no pact, you know." Chris looked pleadingly at M.T., but he knew that he would not be put off. He remembered a movie he had seen about bloodhounds. Once they had been put on the scent there was no getting them off. M.T. was on the scent for sure. The more Chris hesitated, the more eager M.T. was to hear the terrible part.

"We could have a pact, Chris. We could be blood brothers."

Blood brothers! How often he had wished to be blood brothers with M.T. Still he hesitated. "How could we be blood brothers? It would be one sided. We'd mix our blood and I'd tell you my terrible secret, and then what about me? You'd have nothing to tell me."

"Oh, yes, I would." M.T.'s voice was low and deep, and he looked so mysterious Chris wanted to laugh. "I have a terrible secret, too."

Chris could hardly believe his ears. "You have?"

"Yes, it's an old, old one, and I'll tell it to you if you'll tell me yours. Want to be blood brothers?"

27

Of course he did. He'd always wanted to be blood brothers with M.T.

"You know I want to be blood brothers, M.T."

"All right. Get your mom's sewing basket."

"Listen, M.T., I don't want any more trouble with Mom."

"Okay; just get a needle, then."

When Chris returned as fast as he could with a needle, M.T. asked, "Got a match?"

"What do you want a match for?"

"To sterilize the needle."

"Thought you were in a hurry."

M.T. gave him a superior smile. "Not in that much of a hurry."

"Okay." Chris grinned. "I know you're going to be a doctor."

"Well, you're going to the moon; aren't you?"

Chris grinned his yes.

With the precision of a surgeon M.T. pricked Chris' finger with the needle, then squeezed it until the blood appeared. "Hold it," he said to Chris. Then he did the same to his own.

Solemnly they held their fingers together and mixed their blood.

"We are now blood brothers," M.T. intoned. "Now, Chris, tell me your secret. It will be safe with me forever."

Chris wanted to laugh at M.T.'s serious look and the tone of his voice, but he was in a hurry to tell his dread tale, and he could hardly wait to hear M.T.'s secret.

Slowly and trying to minimize it, Chris gave an account of the coming wedding and his part in it.

But M.T. would not have it minimized. At each article of wearing apparel that Chris mentioned M.T. groaned.

At the end of the recital, he put his arm around Chris. "Blood brother, it will remain my deep, deep secret. But your travail will be over in a short time; mine will go on forever."

Chris tried not to grin, but he always found it hard not to when M.T. went on with his fancy words as he was doing now.

"All right. What is your travail?" Chris asked, feeling better already for having told his story.

"Remember your lips are locked on it forever."

"Yes," Chris promised, turning away so M.T. wouldn't see the grin that he could no longer suppress.

M.T. surveyed the entire room quickly, then stepped up close to Chris. "I've carried this burden with me for twelve years now, and I'll carry it forever."

What in the world could he be talking about? Chris watched him closely.

M.T. lowered his voice almost to a whisper. "Chris, have you ever wondered what M.T. stands for?"

"No. It's your name; isn't it? M.T. Jones."

"Chris, M.T. *stands* for my name. Now here it is, and remember, blood brother, you must keep my secret forever. Chris, my name is Malcolm Throckmorton Jones."

"Oh." Chris reeled back. "I'm sorry, M.T."

It was two weeks since Chris and M.T. had exchanged their deep secrets, and a little more than two months until the wedding. The parts for the Columbus assembly had been given out and the High 6th of Room 1 was resigned to its fate. Chris seemed to be in a midstream of existence now. Not once in the last fourteen nights had he jumped from bed to scan the sky, and the only time that he had been sent to the principal's office was to take a message from Miss Foster.

Right now he sat in the classroom and looked at Laurie who was directly in front of him. He studied her long blond ponytail, and bit his lip to keep his grin from flashing. Gently he inched his arm forward and with expert fingers caught the tip of her hair. With the absorption of one completely dedicated to his task, he tied her hair to the back of her belt.

Just as he had it tightly and securely anchored, Laurie turned her head slowly as best she could. "All right now," she whispered, "untie it."

Chris didn't try to keep his grin from flashing. For a girl, Laurie was wonderful.

He didn't give the untying the careful study he had given the tying. Laurie knew what he was doing so there was no need for caution, and he realized that he had missed a great deal of what Miss Foster had been saying. Now he listened intently.

"And so," she was saying in conclusion, "for the remainder of the term, in place of folk dancing we shall have lessons in social dancing to get ready for our High 6th promotion party."

"Social dancing!" Chris called out before he realized what he was doing. "What's that?"

"Chris Muldoon," Miss Foster said, "perhaps you would like to go to the office and have Mrs. Johnstone explain it to you."

"Please, Miss Foster," Chris said to the evident merriment of the class, "I'll take it sight unseen."

But when he saw what it was, Chris found that he hated it. He had always despised Thursday at school because that was folk dancing day. But after twenty minutes of social dancing, folk dancing went soaring in his estimation. There at least you danced in a circle or a square with everybody. In social dancing one boy danced with one girl.

The girls were delighted, and some of the boys

didn't mind, and some of them seemed to be enjoying it as much as the girls were.

But not Chris. He edged away. Miss Foster was so busy getting them in partners and the dancing started that she apparently didn't notice him.

Chris kept backing and backing away until he was almost at the wall of the gym. Just when he was a few steps away from his goal he bumped into someone evidently backing away, too. Chris turned to whisper an apology.

It was M.T.!

"Isn't this awful?" M.T. whispered.

Chris made a wry face and nodded.

They stood side by side and as close to the wall as they could possibly get.

The door to the gym opened abruptly, and Mrs. Johnstone was standing there. M.T. moved quietly toward the dancers. Chris stayed where he was.

"Chris Muldoon, why aren't you dancing?"

Chris started to answer, but Mrs. Johnstone went on, "Remember, young man, there's a place on the report card for this. No dancing means a poor mark in physical education." With that she hurried out of the gym, but to Chris' relief, the recess bell rang just then.

But the day of the first lesson in social dancing seemed to be a milestone in Chris' life. Right that very afternoon Laurie refused to play in the caves after school. She was going to have a group of girls to her house to practice dancing. Chris was half amused, and half disgusted, but he would have been completely disgusted if he could have known that Laurie was never to play in the caves again.

As they walked the few blocks that led to the ocean beach, Chris was amazed when M.T. told him some of the boys hadn't minded the dancing too much. No one had to tell him that the girls just loved it. He saw that for himself.

Now as their feet touched the sands of the beach, Chris raced out as he always did to be the first one to reach the caves of the natural retaining wall that separated the beach from the highway. M.T. followed as usual but it seemed strange without Laurie.

Finally they settled down in the third cave, the largest of all, and their favorite talking place. They mused over the strangeness of things, how in one day so much was changed just because of that old social dancing. Who in the world would ever have thought that Laurie would go for it?

"But even some of the boys don't mind too much," M.T. said.

"Yeh; but Laurie!" Chris' voice was a mixture of amazement and sadness.

Then Chris gave M.T. a sudden suspicious look, but was met with a look of appraisal in return.

"Say," Chris asked, the questioning tone in his voice matching the look in his eyes, "you aren't going to fall for that dancing stuff? Are you?"

M.T. burst out laughing. "I was just about to ask you the same question. You bet I'm not."

He took Chris' hand in a tight clasp. "We're blood brothers; aren't we?"

"Blood brothers we are, and we are not going to dance."

After one more quick hand grasp, and a whoop of glee, each boy quickly took off his shoes and raced to the ocean's edge. They laughed as the foamy water washed over their feet and splashed against their legs. They dug their toes into the wet sand as the waves moved out.

"There they go," M.T. yelled, "Laurie's little fairy ships."

"We certainly teased her enough about them," Chris said. "We didn't let her live that one down."

He stood, using the wet ground as an anchor for his toes, and watched the whitecaps moving in and moving out. When Laurie was little she used to shout, "Look, look! The little fairy ships are drifting out to sea."

When they grew older Chris and M.T. never let

37

her forget it. But that was what was so super about Laurie. She certainly could take teasing.

"How she ever—" Chris started, turning to M.T., but M.T. was already far down the beach.

In a minute, Chris would follow him, but now he surveyed the wide stretch of shore. He, M.T., and Laurie had selected it because it was a secluded part. To the north, were the Cliff House, Seal Rock, the restaurants and the bustle of tourists. To the south, were the rows of motels just across the highway, the hamburger stands, the stores gay with candy apples and cotton candy. This was the place they had selected because not many came here. Sometimes they had it entirely to themselves. These were the days they had the most fun.

He looked out at the enormous ocean stretching far, far to the horizon, and 'way beyond that, he knew.

Gosh, how could Laurie give up all of this just to practice that awful dancing? He stamped up and down, reveling in the cold shock of the water against his legs, and stamped out his reflective mood as well.

"Hey, hey, M.T.," he yelled, "here I come."

He ran along and caught up with his friend.

They rolled their jeans far up over their knees, joined arms and raced out to meet the oncoming breakers, jumping and screaming in delight as the water splashed their feet and pelted against their legs. Then shouting, they ran back to the shore to outwit the receding waves.

They tumbled, and ran, and laughed, and splashed each other, paying no attention at all to Nature who was beginning to gather the magenta-pink, and reddish-gold, and purple that she would later streak across the sky in a display that no artist has ever equalled.

But when the sands began to take on a tinge of gray, and their legs took a little longer to dry after each onslaught of the incoming tide, they knew it was time to leave all these things to the morrow.

But the next day after school when Chris shouted to M.T. as usual, "Race you to the beach," M.T. mumbled something about having to go home first.

There was no need for Chris to run then. He just ambled along the few blocks to the ocean, walked slowly across the sand, and sat outside the cave waiting for M.T. to come, but he didn't arrive.

All the next day at school Chris kept waiting for M.T. to explain, but no explanation came.

At the end of the day Chris' pride wouldn't permit him to say anything to M.T. about the race to the ocean.

He just walked slowly along hoping to be followed, hoping even to find M.T. at the beach when he arrived.

But there was no M.T., and neither did he come.

Chris wandered aimlessly along their old haunts, mising both Laurie and M.T. For the first time in his life, he was caught by an extreme loneliness out here on the deserted beach.

He sifted sand through the fingers of one hand causing it to make a little mound on his other hand.

Well, they had lost Laurie to that old dancing.

Then he sat up startled. M.T.! His own blood brother. Was that why he wasn't coming out here anymore? Was he practicing dancing?

Chris jumped to his feet. There was no longer any loneliness about him. He was sorry about Laurie. With M.T. it was different. Chris' quarter inch of reddish-brown hair fairly bristled. He was going to find out about M.T., and now.

He ran across the sands of the beach, and took up the long city blocks in his urgent stride. He arrived at M.T.'s house before he had really made up his mind what to say, but he had become more angry with each block that he had run.

He rang the bell, and opened his mouth to shout at M.T. the moment the door opened. He was startled and confused to find M.T.'s mother opening the door.

"Oh, Mrs. Jones, is M.T. here?"

"He certainly is, Chris," Mrs. Jones answered, "but he is in his room where he is going to be confined every day after school for the remainder of the week."

All Chris' dark suspicion escaped in one great sigh of relief.

"Oh, I'm so glad," he said.

Mrs. Jones gave him a startled look. "I thought you were M.T.'s friend."

"Oh, I am. I am, Mrs. Jones. It's just that I thought he was somewhere else."

Mrs. Jones bit the smile on her lip. "It's two of a kind you are."

"Thank you, Mrs. Jones," Chris said and jumped down the steps three at a time.

As he passed the side of the house something struck him lightly on the head. He looked up and saw M.T. leaning halfway out his window.

"Psst. Psst, Chris."

Chris went close to the window.

"I know Mom told you I'm grounded," M.T. said. "I was ashamed to tell you myself."

Chris could hardly keep from laughing. M.T. was talking in such loud whispers.

"Chris, come closer still, if you can. I have the most super thing to tell you."

Chris got so close, he practically blended with the building.

"On Tuesdays," M.T. went on, his whisper almost becoming a shout, "Miss Foster is going to teach dancing to Mr. Lawrence's class."

"Well, what's so super about that? It still doesn't let us out of our Thursday dancing."

"No," M.T. said without the slightest note of a whisper. "But when Miss Foster takes his class for dancing, Mr. Lawrence is going to take our class for athletics."

Chris let out such a shout of joy that M.T. said, "Hey, I'm in trouble already," and popped back into the house.

5: Mr. Lawrence

All that kept life from being absolutely perfect was that there was only one Tuesday in the week. How super it was to have Mr. Lawrence for athletics. Not that he was easy. Exactly the opposite. Many a basketball shot that would have had Miss Foster's approval drew Mr. Lawrence's ire.

"You call that's a chest shot?" he would yell. Or, "I say dribble down the court; *dribble*—not tippy-toe."

The boys loved it, and perhaps most of all did M.T. and Chris.

Then the good news came out. Three afternoons a week after school Mr. Lawrence was having basketball for all interested boys in both sixth grades. Besides the excitement and exhilaration of the game, for the first time since Kindergarten they were really rid of Percy. Of course, he didn't go out for basketball.

Then, as if there was no end to good things, Mr. Lawrence announced that he was watching carefully and that in a few weeks he would pick a team and

43

a second string for competitive games with other schools.

That was all that Chris and M.T. needed. They were determined to be on the first string.

"We need extra practice, Chris," M.T. said. "We just have to make that first string."

"I have a basketball," Chris added. "We can practice running and dribbling in my back yard."

"Yeh, that will be fine. But we both need practice in shooting for the basket. If only we had a basketball standard."

If only they had a basketball standard. Chris mulled it over half the morning, his mind only partially on his lessons. Then at arithmetic time when Miss Foster asked him something about measure, intending to answer, "standard measure," he was startled to hear himself answer, "basketball standard."

In the split second that the class burst out in gleeful laughter, the idea came to Chris. He wanted to write a note to M.T., but since he'd already been embarrassed once, he was taking no other chance. He'd wait until recess.

Their feet barely touched the yard at recess when he called to M.T. "I have just the thing. In our basement there's a metal hoop that my father once soldered a little handle onto. If you can get some

of your father's tools, I think we can put the hoop right outside my window."

"Sharpo! Double sharpo!" M.T. shouted. "That is just the thing. Stop at my house on the way from school."

So armed with tools, they found the hoop in Chris' basement and set to work.

After many mishaps the basketball hoop was anchored safely outside Chris' window.

"Mom won't be home for a long time yet," Chris said. "Let's have a little practice."

They took turns, one acting as opposing guard as the other dribbled up the garden path and made a shot for the basket.

"We're getting better and better all the time!" M.T. shouted, slightly out of breath.

Chris came dribbling up the path. "How do you like this for a backward shot?" he yelled. He rose in the air and let go. The ball went sailing in a beautiful arc, but not through the basket. The smashing and shattering and splintering of glass let Chris know that the ball had gone right through his bedroom window.

Almost as if a bell had been rung or a button pushed, Mr. Kitchenger was out yelling, "Ah, I know it's that Chris Muldoon. He's up to some mischief again."

Chris stood for a few minutes in shocked disbelief.

"Gosh, M.T., if Mom finds this out now she won't even let me be on the team."

"How can you keep her from knowing?"

"Oh, I'll tell her eventually. I wouldn't deceive Mom. But if I could only have it fixed before I tell her."

"How are you going to do that? She'll be home soon. You can't get it fixed until tomorrow."

"That's it. If I can just keep her out of my room tonight. I'll pull the shade down. Tomorrow she goes to the hospital to see Dad, and will be gone all day. I always do my own room the day she goes to the hospital. If only I can have it fixed before she comes home. It will be easier to explain to Mom after the window is in."

"Yeh. Have you money?"

"No."

"Haven't you a piggy-bank, or anything?"

"Bank!" The word sent an electric wave to Chris' brain. "Tomorrow is bank day at school. I'll draw some money out of my school account, have the window fixed, explain to Mom, and then gradually earn the money and replace it."

Chris managed to keep Mom out of his room that night and he knew she wouldn't have time the

48

next day, but he was doomed to disappointment when it came to banking.

The next day at recess, bolstered by M.T.'s company, he went into the school library where a bank clerk presided weekly for the children's banking. Yes, Chris learned, the children did their own banking when it came to depositing, but no child could withdraw without his parent's signature.

Two dejected boys left the library and started for the yard.

"What's up with you two?" Mr. Lawrence, who was on yard duty, asked.

M.T. tried to explain while Chris shifted uneasily from foot to foot.

"You aren't trying to deceive your mother; are you, Chris?"

"I never do that, Mr. Lawrence."

Mr. Lawrence laughed and put a reassuring hand on Chris' shoulder. "Your vehemence convinces me, Chris."

He tapped his yard bell at two runners, and said to Chris and M.T., "Come walk around the yard with me while we discuss this. I have a stake in it, too."

"Mr. Lawrence?"

"I don't want to be minus any good players when I pick my first string."

"Mr. Lawrence, you mean Chris?" M.T. asked.

"I mean both of you."

For a minute jubilance seemed to put everything else out of their minds. But Mr. Lawrence brought them back to reality.

"There's that broken window, remember."

They both groaned.

"Do you boys know the most expensive part of repairing a broken window?"

"The glass?" they asked tentatively and together.

"No. The labor, and today, labor is very expensive."

Chris' shoulders slumped and M.T. shuffled unhappily along.

"But," Mr. Lawrence said, "I told you I had a stake in this. I also happen to be a great window repairman."

"You are?"

"Yes. You see, I happened to be the star baseball player on my block; but I also ran up the greatest record for broken windows. At first my dad fixed them, but later he taught me how to repair them. My dad said that the worst part of a broken window was for the one who broke it to run away. He always taught me to ring the doorbell, give my name, and have the window replaced immediately.

Dad would advance the money for the glass, but I always had to return it out of my own earnings."

The boys looked wide-eyed at Mr. Lawrence.

"Chris, I'll buy the glass today, but you'll have to repay me out of your earnings. We'll repair the window right after school."

M.T. and Chris were speechless.

But after school when the three of them entered Chris' bedroom, Mr. Lawrence appeared speechless for a few minutes. Then apparently recovering his voice, he asked, "What have we here?"

He walked around the room, naming the pictures on the wall: "Shephard, Cooper, Glenn, Carpenter, Schirra." He picked up model after model of missiles, launching pads, rockets, capsules.

"What gives?" he asked.

"Oh, Chris is going to the moon," M.T. said.

"So," Mr. Lawrence answered as matter-of-factly as he talked about the window. "You going with him, M.T.?"

"No, Mr. Lawrence. I'm going to be a doctor."

"Well, good. Good for both of you."

Chris looked at Mr. Lawrence, his eyes shining. No teasing, no scoffing. Chris was going to the moon, and Mr. Lawrence believed him.

"We'd better start on that window," Mr. Lawrence said as he removed his coat, shirt and tie.

Chris pulled up the shade to show the broken window.

"Chris, don't tell me you put a basketball hoop right outside a window," the teacher said. "That's just an invitation for breaking."

Mr. Lawrence started to work with a will, the boys acting as eager helpers.

"Some day I'll come by and help you put a basketball standard at the back of the yard."

It was such fun working with Mr. Lawrence, and such a relief to Chris to have the window repaired that time just seemed to fly.

The window was finished and they had just cleaned up the debris when they heard Mom come in.

She walked directly to Chris' room. "I prepared dinner before I left. It won't take long to warm it. Better start getting cleaned up now, boys."

Mr. Lawrence was sitting on the floor between the bed and the window running his finger along the quickly drying putty. Only his dark head and the top of his T-shirt were showing.

He started to rise as Chris mumbled, "Mom, this is Mr. Lawrence."

She was already on her way out before he could get to his feet.

"All right, Lawrence," Mom said, "you may stay

for dinner, too, if it is agreeable to your mother."

Chris stood with his mouth open. M.T. didn't even move.

Mr. Lawrence ran his hand through his dark hair, not much longer than Chris' or M.T.'s. "Chris, Miss Foster wouldn't be very proud of your enunciation. I'm sure your mother didn't hear you say *mister.*"

They were ready for dinner when Mom called. Mr. Lawrence stood behind her chair, holding it for her as she turned from the stove with the last dish.

Her back was to Mr. Lawrence and she said to Chris, "Where is that other boy?"

Chris tried to speak through an agony of embarrassment. "Mom, Mr. Lawrence is there holding your chair for you. Mr. Lawrence teaches Room 2 at Westcliff."

Now it was Mom's turn to be embarrassed. Her face turned pink—not the kind that let Chris know she was angry—but a pink that made her look young and pretty.

"Oh, Mr. Lawrence, Mr. Lawrence, I didn't realize."

"I know, Mrs. Muldoon. After all, I was in my T-shirt, and I was on the floor so you couldn't see how tall I am."

Then Mom apologized for eating in the kitchen.

"When the boys and I are alone, we eat in the kitchen."

"We did that, too, when I was at home, Mrs. Muldoon."

As Mom was removing the salad plates she stood behind him and said, "And you really do look very young, Mr. Lawrence."

"This is my first year of teaching, Mrs. Muldoon. I just received my M.A. and I'm returning for my Ph.D. as soon as I earn enough money. I'm very interested in bioastronautics."

"Bioastronautics!" Chris almost fell off his chair in excitement.

"Finish your dinner, Chris Muldoon," Mom said.

But before dinner was finished she had learned that Mr. Lawrence had gone to colleges in the Midwest, was a star athlete in his undergraduate days, was now living at the YMCA in the city; and had invited him to come often for a home-cooked meal.

When she saw Mr. Lawrence and M.T. to the door, she said, "Now it's not really one of those come-sometime invitations, Mr. Lawrence. Let us make it definitely for Wednesday of next week. If you can get away from all that paper-correcting, leave with Chris and let him show you the ocean. He thinks it is his. I'll have dinner ready when you get here."

When the door closed, Chris turned and looked at Mom. Boy, she was super. He still had to tell her all about the window, but boy, she was super.

And Mr. Lawrence.

Bioastronautics!

6: Spacemen

Chris and M.T. had moaned that Percy had all the luck when he, and not they, was put into Mr. Lawrence's class. Now, however, they were glad that things had turned out as they had. It was really more fun having Mr. Lawrence for athletics, and they could have a different relationship with him than if he was their classroom teacher. For instance, he now called Chris, Astro, and M.T., Doc. Chris laughed at the idea of Miss Foster's doing likewise.

Also there were often things that Chris wished he could talk over with Dad. Now he discussed them with Mr. Lawrence. Too, Chris and Mr. Lawrence had long walks along the beach and many talks on the day each week that Mom made sure that Mr. Lawrence had a home-cooked meal. One couldn't exactly do all these things with a classroom teacher.

On the days they went to the beach alone, Chris and Mr. Lawrence were in the habit of tying the laces of their shoes together, carrying them across their shoulders, rolling up their trousers, and walking along the water's edge, reveling in the feel of wet sand between their toes.

Gradually Mr. Lawrence learned about Dad, Mom, Laurie, Mr. Kitchenger, the lab, Percy at the lab, Chris' aversion to social dancing, the coming wedding. Of course, interlaced through everything was Chris' dream of one day going to the moon.

But there was one thing Chris had held back, but now that he and Mr. Lawrence were on such familiar terms, and he was fast becoming Mr. Lawrence's most promising athlete, he thought he could bring up the matter. He had to do it carefully, he was sure, because he knew that Mr. Lawrence would brook no criticism of Miss Foster.

But Mr. Lawrence himself provided the opening. "It's just tremendous and wonderful, the ocean. You children at Westcliff are certainly fortunate growing up practically on its shores."

"You sound just like Miss Foster," Chris said ruefully. "She'll say, 'you children are growing up right on the shores of the blue Pacific; Columbus played on the shore of Genoa.' Then we know we're going to have a play about Columbus. We've had Miss Foster for three half-years. This is our third play about Columbus."

Chris kicked the wet sand to emphasize his feeling. "We didn't mind the others too much, but this is our last term at Westcliff. This is our most important assembly. And Percy and all the kids in your class are going to have a space program."

Mr. Lawrence laughed and put his arm on Chris' shoulder. "Stay in your orbit, Astro, stay in your orbit."

He guided Chris away from the water. "Here, let's sit a while on the sand, but let's face the ocean. I love to look at the horizon."

Mr. Lawrence scooped up a handful of sand and poured it on Chris' wet feet. "Do you know where I received the idea for my assembly?"

"Where?"

"From Miss Foster."

"Miss Foster!" Chris rose to his feet as he let out a shrill cry.

Mr. Lawrence pulled him down.

"Well, I certainly wish she had kept it for her own class."

"Now listen, Astro, Miss Foster knows that I am interested in space and science. She is interested in history."

"She certainly is," Chris said, going as far as he dared. "Especially Columbus."

Mr. Lawrence quickly shoveled sand with his hands and kept pouring it on Chris' feet making a hasty and improvised tunnel.

"In a way, yours is a space program, too."

"Space program? Columbus space!" Chris threw himself backward on the beach and the sands of the newly made tunnel flew every way.

With one yank, Mr. Lawrence pulled the boy to a sitting position. Still looking at the horizon he said, "Yes, space. Columbus was a spaceman just as much as the astronauts are, just as much as you want to be, Chris."

Chris opened his mouth to protest, but Mr. Lawrence clamped a tight finger over it and went on. "I said *space,* Chris, not outer space. Columbus' space was the wide, blue, unexplored ocean."

Chris' look of protesting disbelief gradually turned into one of amazement.

"And Columbus wasn't the first spaceman, either, Chris. Probably the first spaceman was the one who ventured deepest into the forest, or farthest out on the water near his home."

Chris was listening, his eyes wide with amazement.

Mr. Lawrence smiled at him. "Probably Miss Foster could tell you that the boy Columbus, as he sat on the shores of Genoa, may have had the same look in his eyes as you do when you dream of going to the moon."

Mr. Lawrence stood and started walking toward

the water. As if drawn by a magnet, Chris followed him.

"No man is an island, entire of itself, every man is a piece of the continent, a part of the main. . . ."

Chris could hardly make his tongue move. "Mr. Lawrence, are you quoting poetry?"

Mr. Lawrence stopped and laughed loudly. "It's not poetry. It's very beautiful prose. I learned in English 1A, Chris. You'll have to take 1A yourself someday."

Then he tousled Chris' bristly hair. "Enough of our high-minded talk. I'm hungry. Let's put on our shoes and get going. Your mother probably has dinner waiting for us."

They raced to see who could put his shoes on first; then together they walked across the sands that were slowly turning cool and grayish.

"Three to one your mother has meat pie for dinner," Mr. Lawrence said.

"I'm not taking you up, Mr. Lawrence, because I know what she has for dinner, and it's not meat pie. But boy, it's good, so let's hurry."

As they came within view of Chris' house, Mr. Lawrence whistled. "Say, look at that car outside your house."

"That's not outside my house, Mr. Lawrence. It's outside Mr. Kitchenger's house."

"Boy, boy," Mr. Lawrence said, sounding much like a boy himself, "it's a Monza."

"I don't care what it is," Chris said. "If it's outside Mr. Kitchenger's house, I'm not going near it."

"Probably doesn't even belong to him."

"I'm sure it doesn't. He doesn't even drive. If it's near his house, though, I'm not going near it."

"Oh, come on, Chris. we won't touch it. Let's just look. Isn't it a beauty?"

The sleek black Monza with its fire-red interior was lost on Chris, so great was his fear of Mr. Kitchenger's wrath. If the car had been up the street, Chris would have been in ecstasy about it.

"Look, Chris, look!" Mr. Lawrence was saying.

Chris was proved right, though. From the house came Mr. Kitchenger's shout, "Chris Muldoon, get away from that car and take that young man with you."

"Chris, what are you doing?" Mom called as she opened the door. "Oh, Mr. Lawrence, I didn't know you were with him. I heard Mr. Kitchenger shouting at him. Chris means to be good, but he gets a bit impulsive at times.'

The three of them had a pleasant dinner and talked of many things. They talked of the basketball competition, and Mom brought up the subject of the coming wedding.

Chris groaned. He had been having such a wonderful time lately that the unwelcome thought of the wedding had been crowded from his mind.

"He'll soon have to go for a fitting for his wedding outfit," Mom said.

Chris groaned again.

"What are you moaning about?" Mr. Lawrence asked. "You meet some of the nicest people at weddings."

Then talk of the lab came up, and the award for the competitive examination. Mr. Lawrence told how eager Mrs. Johnstone was to have the honor come to Westcliff School.

"That means," he said, "that either Chris or Percy will have to be the winner."

"I most certainly hope the honor goes to Westcliff, and I hope that my Chris is the one who brings it there."

"He can, too, Mrs. Muldoon," Mr. Lawrence said. Then he laughed. "That is, if he will keep his mind off the moon for a while."

"And will try not to be so forgetful."

But Chris' mind was neither on the moon nor lab right now. It was on the Monza next door, not in the way that Mr. Lawrence was excited about it. Mr. Kitchenger had yelled out to get away from it. That meant Mr. Kitchenger had an interest in it.

If Mr. Kitchenger didn't drive, there must be somebody in his house to whom the Monza belonged.

Who was it?

There was never anybody else in Mr. Kitchenger's house.

There had been so much good talk all evening that Mr. Lawrence left much later than usual.

When Chris went to bed Mom said, "Now it's late, Chris; get into bed and stay there. None of your sky watching tonight."

So Chris didn't dare get out of bed once that he was in it. He was wide awake with curiosity, though. He lay on his stomach, anchored his elbows in the mattress, and held his head up with his two hands.

There were lights in Mr. Kitchenger's house. Was somebody besides Mr. Kitchenger in there?

Finally his head nodded drowsily. He was just about to nod off when two sounds startled him: a garage door being opened, and a motor starting up. Then he could trace the sound as clearly as if he was at the window watching.

The Monza was being driven into Mr. Kitchenger's garage!

Long before his mother called Chris the next morning he was up, dressed, and keeping careful watch on Mr. Kitchenger's house.

Suddenly his pulse accelerated. He had to strain to get a good view. The door to Kitchenger's garage was being opened. Then the Monza was backed out. Chris was sure, without even looking, that Mr. Kitchenger's wasn't in it.

Quickly Chris opened his window and hung halfway out. Now the driver was getting out to close the door. He was tall and lithe and most certainly was not Mr. Kitchenger. According to Chris' quick and inexperienced calculation he was quite a bit older, but still young. If Chris had been the slightest bit interested in such things he would have noticed that the driver of the Monza was quite handsome.

But Chris was interested neither in the man's good looks, nor the sleek sporty look of the car. Chris was sure that something was up. A mystery of some sort.

A mystery!

Now who was better at a mystery than M.T.? The blood of a sleuth ran through his veins.

That was it. M.T. would have to stay with Chris tonight. Then the two of them would keep careful watch on the house next door.

Now the blood raced through Chris' veins. He and M.T. had often kept watch on Mr. Kitchenger's house in a vague indefinite way. This was something real. Something, he knew, that M.T. would say, "to put your teeth into."

Now, all that he had to do was to get M.T. to stay tonight. The first step in that was in Mom's direction. She had to be softened up.

He was all dressed. He knew! He'd make his bed and tidy his room. He set to with a will. He was just about finished when Mom opened his door, calling, "Chris, Chris, time to get up."

Then she stopped in amazement. "All dressed, and your room cleaned. Why, Chris, sometimes you do surprise me. But there is one more thing. I want you to change into your slacks and good jacket."

"Mom?"

"You heard me. You change. I'll get breakfast. I'll explain while we're eating.

He was slower at getting changed than he was at getting completely dressed. Gee, what was up? Why did he have to wear good slacks and his best jacket to school?

But Mom told him the minute that breakfast started.

"Chris, I'll meet you after school. I've decided that we'd better go today to pick out your wedding outfit, in case there should have to be some alterations."

"Oh, gosh, Mom, do I have to?"

"Remember you made the bargain. You haven't forgotten the incident of the rope ladder, and the shooting, and the police sirens; have you?"

Chris reddened. "No, Mom." He ate the mush which he hated and usually protested about without a word. But finally he said, "But gee, Mom, the bus stop is a block from school. Couldn't you meet me there instead of right in front of the building?"

There was a twinkle in her eye that Chris didn't see because he was miserably contemplating his unfinished mush. "Well of course, Christopher," she said, "if you are so ashamed of your mother, I'll meet you a block away."

Now Chris was all sincere contrition. "Mom, Mom, it's not that at all. I just didn't want any of the kids to see me. Suppose they'd guess where I was going."

"How could they ever guess? Did you tell any of them you were going to be in a wedding party?"

"Just M.T. and he's sworn to eternal secrecy."

"How could anybody else guess then?"

"Mom, it's just the thought is so obnoxious to me, I'm afraid that in some mysterious way the knowledge has become a common one."

She was trying to control the little smiles that chased each other around her lips. "I must say that Miss Foster is doing wonders with your vocabulary."

Finally she said, "Come on now, Chris, finish your breakfast. It's almost time to go. I'll meet you at the bus stop right after school. It won't be so bad, Chris."

When he had finished, she went to the door with him, and put his lunch box in his hand at the last minute.

"What is it, Moon Man?" she asked. She let her eyes travel affectionately from the stubble of reddish-brown hair, to the green eyes, the growing boy neatly but reluctantly dressed in good jacket and slacks. "What is it that you want to ask me?"

"Mom?"

"Surely you didn't get up early and clean your room just out of a feeling of charity."

Chris laughed and looked sheepishly at his mother. It was pretty hard to fool her.

"Well, Mom, I was going to ask you something, but going downtown after school changes things."

"How? What were you going to ask me?"

Chris opened and closed the snaps on his lunch box repeatedly. "I ... I was going to ask you if M.T. could stay tonight. But since ..."

"Oh, we'll be home in time for dinner. I'll prepare it this morning and will just have to heat it. Surely M.T. may come for dinner and stay all night. It may soften the blow."

Chris put his lunch box on the floor and hugged his mother. "Gee, Mom, you're super. Really super."

It did soften the blow. The minute he put his foot in the schoolyard, Chris looked for M.T., but his friend didn't come running into the yard until the bell rang. Chris would have to wait until recess and he found it hard, indeed.

M.T. evidently sensed it. As soon as they reached the yard for recess he said, "What gives, Chris? I can tell there's something up. Has it anything to do with your fancy clothes?"

"No," Chris laughed ruefully, and then lowered his voice to a whisper. "I have to go downtown with Mom after school and be measured for that horrible old wedding outfit. Remember you are sworn to secrecy."

M.T. gave him a tight handclasp. "Blood brother," he said solemnly.

Then Chris told him just enough about the Monza and Mr. Kitchenger's visitor to get the sleuth in M.T. really ready for action.

"Mom says you may come for dinner and stay all night. Then we can really detect things."

M.T. let out a joyous whoop. "I have to check with my mother after school, but I'm sure she'll let me."

Every time Chris looked at M.T. he was met with shiny-eyed eagerness, so he went through the day without too much worry about what would happen after school.

He held his breath, though, as he walked the one block to the bus. To his relief Mom was there and he reached the corner just as the bus pulled up. No one he knew was waiting for it. Quickly he helped her on. He gave a hasty survey to the bus. There were just two vacant seats, and he escorted her to one and sat beside her. He breathed easier. At least no one at school would know where he was going.

Just as the bus started someone shouted, "Wait. Oh, please wait."

The accommodating driver obliged and stopped the bus.

Laurie boarded the bus! Now where in the world did she come from?

Chris tried to shrink into his place, but evidently Laurie had seen them immediately.

"Oh, Mrs. Muldoon," she said. "Hi, Chris."

Mom turned to Chris, but he was already on his feet giving his seat to Laurie.

"Where are you going?" Laurie asked, her voice all friendly and not the least bit prying.

But Chris turned several shades of red and seemed unable to find his tongue.

"To Jenning's Men's Store," Mom said and stopped.

Chris sent her a look of deepest gratitude. Mom was swell.

"How nice your hair looks, Laurie," she said. Then she turned to Chris. "You didn't tell me that Laurie had her ponytail cut."

Chris gave Laurie a startled look. Her soft blond hair was shoulder length and turned under, and soft little curly bangs lined her forehead.

"I didn't know she had it cut," he mumbled in confusion.

Laurie laughed lightly. "Chris hasn't really looked

at me since I stopped playing in the caves at the beach and since the class started social dancing."

Mom gave Chris an amused look.

To his relief Laurie left the bus before they did. But the relief was only temporary. He and Mom were soon in Jenning's Men's Store with Chris being fitted for the wedding outfit. Each article of apparel was a new indignity. But the worst of all came when Chris was fully outfitted and the salesman insisted that he stand in front of the full-length mirror.

Chris took one look at himself and groaned as the salesman stood clucking admiringly beside him.

Mom was smiling as if she, too, thought that he looked well.

There was only one thing about the whole awful experience that really was good. Alterations were needed, so at least he wouldn't have to take the outfit home with him tonight.

Then, of course, there was the expectation of his coming nocturnal watch with M.T.

All in all, the bus trip back home was much more pleasant than the one downtown had been.

8: *Ah Ha!*

Chris didn't even mention the trip downtown to M.T. In fact, painful as it had been to him, he gave it very little thought. All he could think of was getting through dinner, finishing homework, and going, allegedly, to bed. He could tell that M.T. was on edge, too. Chris felt safe from his mother's discerning eye because he knew that she would charge everything to the unhappy experience about the wedding outfit.

As soon as they safely could, they bade her good night and went into the bedroom. They actually did get undressed and into bed, Chris in the lower bunk, M.T. in the upper. But they really were taking up observation posts.

They lay for a long time absolutely quiet. Then Chris whispered urgently, "M.T., there's a light in Kitchenger's house, not in Mr. Kitchenger's room. It's in the other one."

M.T.'s whisper could be heard all over the room. "I can see a man sitting at a table."

"I can't see from here."

"Come on up," M.T. said, talking and moving over at the same time.

Chris, a veteran at climbing into bunk beds, was there in a minute. "That's the man I saw in the Monza. M.T., what's he doing? He has papers spread over the table and he is studying them very closely."

"They're blueprints or specifications of some sort."

"Are you sure, M.T.?"

"Sure, I'm sure. Haven't I seen my dad with them many times?"

Chris' voice was a hollow whisper. "Specifications of what, I wonder. Do you suppose it has anything to do with our moon probe? Do you suppose he's working to sabotage . . . ?"

"Oh, Chris, you and that moon flight. It could be perfectly innocent, like my dad bringing blueprints and specifications home to give them extra study."

The moon that Chris hoped one day to explore cast its silvery light upon the upper bunk and in that softened glow Chris looked sadly and accusingly into M.T.'s eyes. What in the world was he doing to their mystery?

"Yeh," Chris went on, his voice as sad as his eyes, "in any house but Kitchenger's. You know Mr. Kitchenger."

M.T. squirmed and apparently caught hold of

himself. After all he was the chief sleuth of the duo; he was the one who loved a mystery more than anything.

He reached out and gave Chris the hand grasp. "Blood brother, I understand. In any house but Kitchenger's. Let us give this man and his deeds our most minute scrutiny."

Chris chuckled to himself for two reasons. He never could resist laughing at M.T.'s grand words, and grander manners. Then he laughed, too, in relief. Suppose his beautiful mystery came to nothing?

"Yes, we must watch minutely. On your elbows, Chris."

They both lay on their stomachs, chin in hand, propped up by their elbows. They watched every move that the man next made. Slowly, carefully, exactly, he pored over the papers on the table. Slowly, carefully, and for hours.

Gradually each boy nodded and dozed. Then finally one and then the other fell off into a deep sleep.

And that was where Mom found them in the morning.

"Now can anyone tell me," she asked of no one in particular, "why both want to sleep in the same bunk, and in the upper one at that?"

Of course, Chris couldn't possibly have M.T. stay night after night, so they decided that Chris would watch each night, and report to M.T. in the morning. If anything really important happened they would somehow manage to have M.T. stay overnight again.

The next night and the next were exactly the same. The man seemed to spend the whole night just studying the papers. But after the third night Chris had a little more to report. He was writing and drawing. "He was using those things your father does when he measures and draws circles and things," Chris added.

"Oh, protractor and triangle," M.T. said knowingly. "Hum," he added, "hum." He squinted his eyes and ran his hand slowly through his stubble of blond hair. "Hum..."

"What do you mean, *hum?*" Chris asked.

"Hum," M.T. repeated, his eyes practically closed this time.

Chris looked at him quizzically. Did he really know something or was he just putting on his detective act?

But the next day Chris really had something to report. Even though he had stayed awake as long as he could last night, watching his suspect drawing, measuring, writing, he was wide awake the minute the motor of the Monza started up, and at the window as soon as it was backed out of the garage.

Then, as M.T. would have said, he struck pay dirt. As the Monza made a right into the street and started off, a large binder-size piece of paper flew out and lodged against a power pole.

In a minute Chris had his rope ladder anchored, climbed down, ran to the power pole and retrieved the paper.

He dashed back into his room without even looking at it. Gosh, if Mom ever again caught him on the street in his pajamas! He remembered his first night on the rope ladder. That incident was the cause of his having to be in the wedding.

The wedding! This coming Sunday was the day.

But even the imminent horror of the wedding couldn't hold his thoughts for long. The paper. He must study it. Carefully he spread it out on his bed. The map of California—evidently hand drawn and carefully done. At different places on the map were red circles, each labeled with a carefully printed name.

He ran his finger along the circles. Halfway up the coast he spotted the word *Vandenberg*. He knew it was an air force base. Then he spotted *Travis*.

Another air-force base. He purposely looked on the map for the area around the Mojave Desert. He knew what was at that location. There it was, printed as neatly and clearly as the others. *Edwards!* Edwards Air Force Base had been selected as the training center for the future astronauts.

Now Chris knew that he was on to something. Even as the words, *Castle, March, Beale* danced before his eyes, he started dressing. In no time he grabbed the map and started off. He wouldn't go straight to school; he'd stop and call for M.T. They could talk along the way.

He dashed out of the house. The front door was hardly closed behind him, when it was opened again. Mom was standing there.

"Chris Muldoon, I declare, you have forgotten everything under the sun one time or another, but this is the first time I have ever known you to forget your breakfast. Will you please come in here while it is still hot?"

"Gosh, Mom, gosh." Abashed, Chris walked into the house and to the table.

He forced a few bites down. "Mom, I'm not really hungry."

"Well, eat your breakfast regardless. From the look of you I know you are on the start of some great endeavor. You need good warm food to give you strength."

He forced some more of his breakfast down. "Mom, how many of the air-force bases in California can you name?"

She puzzled for a moment. "None that I can think of." She urged another piece of toast on him. "Oh, yes, there is one. Edwards, where they train the future astronauts. I know someone who is going to the moon some day." She sent him a teasing look. "And that someone had better be on his way to school right now."

"Okay, Mom." He gave a quick peck to her cheek.

"And Chris," she called after him, "please try not to be so forgetful."

"All right, Mom."

In the middle of the block he stopped and ran back.

"What did you forget now?"

"Mom, may M.T. stay tonight? We have something very important to discuss."

"If Mr. Lawrence can stand the both of you," she answered. "He's coming to dinner tonight."

"Of course, he can stand us. He has thirty-six kids all day."

"That's what I was thinking of," Mom said.

He couldn't stop for M.T. now. It was too late.

As usual, M.T. reached school just as the bell rang. Chris would have to wait until recess. But so many looks passed between the two of them, Chris was sure that M.T. knew something was up. He had what Chris called his bloodhound look.

Finally the recess bell rang, but they came close to not having any play. M.T. evidently just could not wait until they reached the yard. He maneuvered so that he was right behind Chris in line.

"What is it, Chris? What? What? I know you have something."

"Tell you in the yard," Chris mumbled out of the side of his mouth.

As this tiny conversation was going on, the line had progressed along the hall until it was just opposite Mrs. Johnstone's office. Now she appeared at her door. Every child at Westcliff knew that quiet lines were very important to Mrs. Johnstone. Chris could tell how eager the sleuth in M.T. must be for him even to dare to talk outside Mrs. Johnstone's door.

But Miss Foster came up in her gentle way as she so often did and spoke quietly to Mrs. Johnstone, so a difficult situation passed.

The minute they reached the yard, M.T. started in. "Chris, hurry, hurry, I know you have something to tell me."

Chris was tempted to take a leaf out of M.T.'s own book, and he gave into his urge briefly.

"I not only have something to tell you, I also have something to show you." M.T. could have hardly done better, himself.

"Chris, Chris, come on! Come on!"

"Let's go to the side of the building where we won't be bothered."

Chris produced the map, and then minutely and step by step reported every happening and every detail of last night, and this morning.

Even in his own excitement he almost had to laugh at M.T. His pal's eyes were as wide and round as large buttons, and so was his mouth.

"We'll have to report it," M.T. said solemnly.

"To the police?"

"No. No. To the F.B.I."

The bell calling for return to class cut off M.T.'s important air. But he did take time to say, "Right after school."

They weren't in the classroom very long when a messenger came in and gave a note to Miss Foster. She read it and called for class attention.

"This is a note from Mr. Lawrence," she said. "Even though today isn't a regular practice day, he would like to meet with the basketball teams because he has very important news for them."

Chris' and M.T.'s eyes met. What would normally have been great excitement to them now became consternation.

What would they do about the F.B.I.?

9: Mr. Lawrence Solves the Mystery

When the basketball team met in the gym after school, Chris could tell immediately that something was up. He had rarely seen Mr. Lawrence so excited.

"Well, boys," he said, "we've made it. We're in the all-city elementary basketball league."

He was immediately drowned out by the cheers of the boys.

He lifted his hands for silence. "We play Polk School first. I hope we go on playing until we reach the finals, and bring the banner home to Westcliff."

The cheers lifted to the rafters of the gymnasium.

"By the way, our practice will have to be accelerated. Every day now, boys, beginning Monday, every single day."

Today it seemed that Mr. Lawrence couldn't say a thing without being cheered.

"Now, though today isn't a regularly scheduled practice, since you're all here, I'll give some pointers you're going to need in any competitive game."

Mr. Lawrence walked to the box and took a basketball.

"Now it's all right for anyone who wishes to leave. You may have something you have to do. After all, you didn't know I was going to call this extra session. Anyone want to leave?"

No one moved.

There was a mixed chorus of "No, Mr. Lawrence, I don't have to leave"; "I can stay"; "Golly, I want to stay."

Chris' and M.T.'s glances crossed. M.T. mouthed the words, "F.B.I."

Chris, a veteran of many a dilemma, sat there seething through this one. He certainly loved basketball, and without being the least bit conceited about it, he could tell that Mr. Lawrence considered him one of his best players. But what about the matter that he and M.T. had to take up with the F.B.I.? He couldn't forget it, although he tried to give all his attention to Mr. Lawrence. Was M.T. having the same trouble?

Chris stole a sideward glance at him. M.T. was looking at Mr. Lawrence as if he hadn't a thought in the world except basketball. For a minute Chris stared in disbelief. M.T.'s eyes had been just as round and button-like this morning when Chris had shown him the map.

Then in a rare flash of understanding he somehow realized that to him, Chris, the map represented a threat to the moon flight—the moon that he watched so carefully every night from its fragile crescent-like beginning to its glorious fullness, and then its nightly waning until once again only the silver crescent graced the sky.

Chris knew he was trapped now. He'd have to stay. He knew he would be able to arouse M.T.'s excitement again on the way home. They'd have plenty of time to call the F.B.I. before Mr. Lawrence came for dinner.

But there again he was met with disappointment. When Mr. Lawrence gave the word for dismissal, and the boys started out of the gym, he called to Chris.

Chris pulled M.T. along with him.

"Chris"—Mr. Lawrence was still bubbling over with enthusiasm—"I'm going to your house for dinner tonight, you know. Wait until I clean up. Then we'll walk together."

"I'm going to be there, too, Mr. Lawrence," M.T. said. "I'm staying at Chris' house all night."

"Good. The three of us can walk together."

The two boys sat waiting, Chris, a picture of dejection; M.T., all eager excitement.

"Boy, Chris, we're lucky. We can do extra talking about basketball to Mr. Lawrence."

Chris stared him in the eye. "M.T., sometimes I

wonder why I have you for my best friend, and my blood brother at that."

"What's the matter with you?"

Chris' face became red to the roots of his stubbly hair. "Why did I run back this morning in all my excitement and beg Mom to let you stay tonight?"

M.T. rose to his feet as if propelled by an electric shock. "The map! The F.B.I., Chris, I forgot. I'm sorry. I was so carried away by the idea of the basketball league. Honestly, Chris, I'm sorry."

Chris stood, his face still red, his lips pressed close together.

"I'll make it up." M.T. reached out and gave him the hand grasp. "Honestly, blood brother, I'll make it up to you."

"What are you going to make up?" Mr. Lawrence, jacket on, tie in place, was standing grinning at them. "What big crisis did I walk in on?"

There was nothing to do but tell him, first one talking, then the other filling in the forgotten details until they came to the dramatic moment when Chris thrust the map into Mr. Lawrence's hands.

They stood breathless while he examined it. Then still holding the map he said to them, "So you think you found a spy."

"Oh, yes," M.T. said. "It definitely has to do with

the air force. But Chris is afraid that the moon flight is being sabotaged. There's an extra mark near Edwards. You know, the future astronauts are trained at Edwards, and we think that the spy . . ."

"Spies, you mean, not spy. Spies."

"Spies, Mr. Lawrence. You think that there are more than one?"

"I know there are." Mr. Lawrence's voice was as stern as it ever was at yard duty when someone had broken an important rule. "Two spies. Two rude, impudent boys daring to invade their neighbor's privacy night after night, sitting in the dark of their own room, looking into their unsuspecting neighbor's lighted room and spying on his every movement."

"But, Mr. Lawrence . . ."

"Chris, does your mother know about this?"

"No, Mr. Lawrence."

"Of course not. I don't know why I even bothered to ask such a question. Now the only decent thing for you to do, Chris, is to return the map that you found."

"Oh, Mr. Lawrence, I wouldn't dare go into Mr. Kitchenger's house. In fact, I don't think he'd let me in."

"Well, Chris." Now the anger was gone from Mr. Lawrence's voice and a little of the teasing look was just coming into his eyes. "I can't say that I blame him. I'll leave your house early tonight and take it in myself."

Dinner was a strange affair. Only Mom acted as if everything was the same as usual. The after-dinner conversation seemed to be a little strained, too, with Mom apparently the only one who didn't notice.

As soon as he gracefully could, Mr. Lawrence excused himself because of pressing business. Chris and M.T. didn't look at each other.

Mr. Lawrence had just about time enough to reach the house next door when Chris loudly invited M.T. into his room to see the model of a missile that he had recently finished.

They stood together in the dark room.

"I'll put the light on in a minute and show you the missile, M.T." He lowered his voice. "I wonder what's going to happen?"

"I don't know. Look! The light just went on in Kitchenger's house. Oh, there's the Monza man and Mr. Lawrence walking to the table where all the papers are spread out."

Mr. Lawrence's angry words about spies were only a few hours old, the strained conversation at dinner was just minutes away, yet the two boys joined hands and as if drawn by a magnet walked to the window of the darkened room.

Just as they reached their destination they saw Mr. Lawrence standing in the lighted window of the house next door. Slowly, deliberately, he pulled the shade to the very bottom of the window.

Chris pressed the light switch.

M.T. took a coin from his pocket. "I'll toss you for the lower bunk."

In the morning Chris found it good to have M.T. in the lower bunk. They could start their conjecturing immediately. They had plenty of time to do so, too, for they didn't see Mr. Lawrence all morning.

"I really don't know if I want to see him or not," Chris confided to M.T.

"Same here," M.T. joined in.

But their decision was made for them just before the noon recess when a messenger arrived with a note for Miss Foster.

"Chris and M.T.," she said after she read it, "Mr. Lawrence would like to see both of you in his room at twelve-thirty."

Now the conjecturing reached its full height. They spent the whole period from twelve to twelve-thirty nibbling at their food and wondering just what would take place when they reached his room.

When they went into his classroom they could see that he was not angry, but he sounded very serious.

"Well, I've solved the mystery, boys. With your

help, of course." Then he said, most solemnly, "The man turned out to be a cartographer."

M.T. reeled back. "A cartographer! A cartographer!"

Chris looked at M.T. in amazement. How did he know all about it? Chris had never even heard the word before.

"Now shall we call the F.B.I., Mr. Lawrence?"

"No."

For a minute, Chris thought that he saw a little twinkle in the teacher's eyes, but he must have imagined it.

"No," Mr. Lawrence went on sternly, "I suggest that both of you go to that bookcase, take a dictionary and look up the word, *cartographer*. I'll write it here on the board because I'm sure that neither of you sleuths knows how to spell it."

They both found the word at the same second, and in unison and amazement read, "A maker of maps or charts."

"Exactly, and that is precisely what Mr. Kitchenger's nephew is doing. By the way, he is Mr. Kitchenger's nephew.

"Bart Kitchenger (that's the nephew's name) is making maps for a book that is coming out, and unlike two friends of mine, he does it precisely, carefully, scientifically. Most fascinating. He studies the terrain (need your dictionaries again?) on foot and by helicopter and plane. Most interesting. While he is working in this area, he stays in his uncle's house.

"By the way, boys, you did me a great favor. Did you ever notice this little gold key I wear? Well, Bart Kitchenger has one, too. Even though we went to different colleges, it means we belong to the same fraternity. And guess what happened? Last night he gave me a ride in his Monza!"

Affectionately he tousled both stubbly heads at once. "Sorry I spoiled your mystery, boys. But now you'll be able to put your whole mind on basketball."

"Beginning Monday," M.T. said. "Chris still has to get through that wedding Sunday."

"Cheer up, Chris," Mr. Lawrence said, "You may meet some very interesting people at the wedding."

10: Rehearsal

The last thing Mr. Lawrence had mentioned yesterday was the wedding, when he teasingly told Chris that he might meet some interesting people there. Now the wedding was the very first topic that Mom brought up this morning at breakfast.

"You have basketball practice this afternoon, don't you, Chris?"

"Yes, Mom." Between that answer and Mom's next sentence Chris flashed his thoughts quickly to Mr. Lawrence. How would he be today? Would he say anything to M.T. and Chris?

A strange sensation centered in the pit of his stomach, and he felt the red of embarrassment start to creep into his face. He was glad to concentrate on Mom.

"Now, hurry home as soon as the practicing is over. You have to have a haircut, bathe, dress and be ready for the rehearsal at seven."

"Rehearsal? What rehearsal?"

"The wedding rehearsal."

"What's a wedding rehearsal?"

"Practice for the wedding. You have rehearsals for your plays at school; don't you?"

"Sure, Mom."

"Well, people have rehearsals for their weddings, Chris. Especially for their weddings."

"But why do I have to go tonight, Mom?"

"Because you are going to be in the wedding party on Sunday."

"Can't I just wait until Sunday?"

"Do you know what to do at a wedding? What are you going to do Sunday?"

"I don't know, Mom. I didn't think of it. I try not to think of that wedding at all."

She poured another glass of milk for him. "Chris, stop being so ridiculous and finish your breakfast. The wedding rehearsal will be held tonight so that everyone will know what to do. One of Bob's friends will call for you."

"Who's Bob?"

"The man your cousin Pamela is going to marry. There will be a best man and three ushers beside yourself. They are all friends of Bob; understand?"

"Yes, Mom."

"One of them will call for you after dinner to take you to the rehearsal."

Chris took one last chance. "Gosh, Mom, do I have to go?"

"Yes," she said emphatically. "And, Christopher, I am getting a little exasperated with you."

He knew she was by the sound of her voice and the two round pink spots on her cheekbones. He grabbed his lunch box, gave her his usual quick peck, and started for the door.

"I'll leave the minute practice is over, Mom." He used his most placating tone.

He swung his lunch box idly as he walked slowly to school. He surely hoped that Mr. Lawrence wasn't exasperated with him, too.

He found that M.T. also was worried. In fact, M.T. was already there when Chris arrived. When M.T. was early for school that certainly meant something.

"Hey, Chris," he said. "How do you think Mr. Lawrence will be today at practice?"

"I don't know, M.T. I was wondering about it, too. Still he was friendly enough when we left him yesterday."

"Yeh. There are many problems though; aren't there, Chris? Mom says I make most of them myself."

"You think you have problems." Chris' expression

95

was filled with self-pity. "Do you know what I have to do tonight? I have to go to a wedding rehearsal. As if it isn't bad enough to have to be in the wedding, I have to practice for it tonight."

"Gosh." M.T. gave him a look that was all blood-brotherly sympathy. "And do you have to wear all those fancy clothes tonight?"

Chris was stopped cold at the enormity of the thought. "Golly, I don't know. I forgot to ask Mom."

Two dejected boys walked into the classroom at the sound of the bell.

Chris felt that he just could not stand one more thing. But as he was leaving the room after school on his way to basketball practice, Miss Foster stopped him.

"Chris, I know you are so interested in basketball, and that is fine, but you are not easing up on your studies at the lab; are you?"

"No, Miss Foster." He looked at her in surprise. Why did she bring that up now?

She answered him in her next remark. "The competitive examination is drawing close. Mrs. Johnstone is so eager to have the honor come to Westcliff. She doesn't mind whether you or Percy brings the award. She just hopes that it comes to Westcliff. I want it to come to Westcliff, too; but Chris, as your teacher, I hope that you are the one who brings it."

Chris was so surprised he didn't know what to say.

"Hurry to your practice now, Chris," Miss Foster urged him on.

"Do you think I give too much time to basketball practice, Miss Foster?"

"Oh, no, Chris. Exercise and play are good for you. Hurry now."

Chris did hurry to the gym, but on the way he pondered just how complicated things could become, especially for Chris Muldoon.

Mr. Lawrence acted as if there had never been any mystery at all, that he had never scolded the boys for spying on their neighbors. His enthusiasm for the game was all that seemed to matter.

"Mom says," M.T. offered on the way home, "that good teachers never hold anything in. They scold kids just when they need it, and that's that."

"Well, Mr. Lawrence certainly is the best," Chris said.

"He surely is," M.T. agreed. He walked as far as Chris' house, then left him with a "good-bye" and another blood-brotherly look of sympathy.

Chris felt that same sensation in the pit of his stomach again. But Mom's greeting was some help.

"Good, right on time, Chris. That shows you are beginning to take responsibility."

"Mom?"

"Never mind," she went on busily. "Hurry in, have a glass of milk, and then go on to the barber's for your haircut."

She saw him to the door. "Keep up your good work. No dawdling now. Remember one of Bob's friends will call for you at seven."

Chris received his haircut without incident except that he had a bad moment when Gus, the barber, asked why he was having a haircut on Thursday instead of Saturday.

Chris squirmed his way out of that one with a laconic, "I don't know."

He was still in his mother's good graces when he arrived home.

"You made fine time, Chris. I'll lay your things out for you."

"Mom, do I have to wear those wedding things tonight?"

Mom laughed. "Not tonight, Chris. Wear your good slacks and best jacket."

Just then the bell rang, and Chris went to answer it. Standing there was a young man about six feet tall, dressed in slacks and sports jacket. His dark hair was cut as short as Chris'. He had friendly

2979

brown eyes and a matching smile. He offered his hand. "I'm Jack Reynolds. You must be Chris."

Just then Mom arrived at the door and Jack Reynolds introduced himself and explained that there'd been a change of plans, that he had to go to the airport to meet one of the ushers, and wondered if he could take Chris with him now, pick up his friend at the airport, and then go right to the rehearsal.

"But Chris hasn't had his dinner yet."

"Neither have I, Mrs. Muldoon." Chris could see that the friendly smile was winning Mom.

"As soon as we pick up Ken," he went on seeming sure of her agreement, "we'll stop at a drive-in for a hamburger."

"All right. Hurry and change, Chris."

"He looks all right to me right now, Mrs. Muldoon," Jack Reynolds said in his pleasant way. He turned to Chris. "Just get your jacket, fella."

Chris looked at his mother, and to his surprise, she laughed and nodded her consent.

The nearer they got to the airport, the less formidable the thoughts of the wedding and the rehearsal became. If Jack Reynolds didn't mind being in the wedding party, why should he? He certainly liked Jack Reynolds. Anything he did was okay with Chris.

"It sure will be good to see old Ken again," Jack said. "The three of us haven't seen him for five months."

"The three?" Chris questioned.

"Yeah. Bob, Bill and I. The three of us flew in from Travis this morning, but . . ."

Chris interrupted him. "Travis? That's an air-force base; isn't it?"

"Sure is." He saluted smartly. "Lieutenant Jack Reynolds at your service, sir."

"The air force!" Chris liked even the feel of the words on his tongue. "You're a lieutenant in the air force?"

"Sure," Jack said. "Couldn't tell without the uniform, uh? So are Bob and Bill and Ken. Ken will have his uniform on when we meet him. He couldn't make the right connections for an air-force plane, so he had to take a commercial one. He was to leave the base right for the plane, so I'm sure he'll be in uniform. Boy, it will be good to see old Ken again."

"Where has he been?"

"Oh, didn't I tell you? He was transferred to Edwards five months ago."

"Edwards?" Chris was so excited he could hardly mouth the words. "Edwards! That's the Flight Test Center, isn't it?"

"You're sure up on stuff, fella."

"Isn't that where they are training some of the astronauts of the future?"

"Sure is, fella." Jack's pride showed in his voice. "Why do you think they transferred old Ken?"

Maybe a future astronaut, and he was to meet him in a few minutes. Then suddenly Mr. Lawrence's words came into Chris' mind, "You may meet some very interesting people at the wedding."

Well, he had certainly met an interesting person when Jack Reynolds rang his doorbell. And now they were on their way to the airport to meet Jack's friend, Ken, probably a future astronaut.

Suppose Mom had let him off? Suppose he hadn't been in the wedding? He would have missed all this.

11: The Wedding

As Chris dressed for the wedding, he thought back over the past weeks and all the events that led to this day: his absolute horror when Mom had first told him about his part in the wedding, his dread of telling M.T., and his fear that anyone he knew would see him in his wedding outfit.

Well, now he wished M.T. could see him. He would like everyone to see him. He donned each part of his outfit with pride. Just think of being dressed like Jack and Bob and Bill and Ken. That's what Mom had said when she first told him about the wedding. She said that he would dress like every usher in the wedding party.

How happy he was to do that now. How wonderful to be in the same party with Jack and Bob and Bill, but especially Ken who might be a future astronaut. All four of them had been so nice to him at rehearsal last night, and at Pamela's house later. He could hardly wait to see them again.

He was ready even before his mother, and went into the living room to wait for her. He sat carefully on the overstuffed chair. He was sure that his four new airmen friends would be dressed with meticulous care. Even in their sports clothes last night he noticed how well-groomed they looked as they walked up the aisle in rehearsal. He certainly wanted to be just like them.

He heard Mom calling as she walked toward his room, "Chris, Chris, hurry now. It's almost time."

"I'm here, Mom, in the living room," he called.

Then he could hear her coming along the hall, her heels tapping out the staccato of her voice. "Chris Muldoon, I declare, if you are in there up to some of your nonsense when you should be getting ready for the wedding, I declare that the minute we reach home you . . ."

With that she reached the living room, and Chris rose exactly as he had seen Bob rise when Pamela entered the room last night.

Mom stood, her lips parted, and looked at Chris as if she really couldn't believe it was he.

"Why, Christopher!" she said.

Chris was glad to hear the bell ring just then.

"I'll answer it, Mom. It must be Jack calling for us." Chris dashed to the door and yanked it open.

"Well, well," Jack said, eying Chris from head to toe, "wait 'til the girls see you."

But Chris was standing, his mouth open, his whole face a study of disappointment. Jack was wearing his air-force uniform.

"Are you ready for the wedding?" Chris asked, clinging to one little bit of hope.

"Just as ready as you are, fella," Jack said heartily.

"But I thought ... Mom said ..."

Then Chris remembered exactly what she had said, "Like every young usher in a wedding party." That made quite a difference.

"Are you all wearing your uniforms?"

"Sure, and proudly. Just as you are wearing your uniform."

"Uniform? What uniform?"

Jack took hold of the lapel of Chris' white jacket. "This is your uniform ... your wedding uniform."

That certainly made a difference. He and Mom had been calling it a wedding outfit. He squared his shoulders and looked proudly at Jack. Whatever his uniform, he would be in the wedding march with Jack and Bob and Bill, but especially with Ken.

He did wear it proudly.

The music started, and the stirring and craning of the guests let the ushers and best man know that the bride had arrived at the church door. With the other men of the wedding party Chris stood at the side front of the church. He would be the leader. He would have to walk across the front of the church, and meet Penny in the middle aisle just before she reached the altar rail.

He started proudly, knowing that the airmen were following him. He even looked at Penny as he met her and offered his arm. (He hadn't looked at her during the rehearsal.)

She was dressed in pale-green with a wreath of pink roses in her short nondescript-brown hair. Suddenly he found himself thinking of Laurie's new hair-do that Mom had called to his attention. He was so startled, he almost stubbed his toe on the altar step as he entered the sanctuary.

The girls walked to the left, the men to the right. He didn't have to look at Penny anymore. He didn't pay much attention to the bride, either. He just stood tall and proud with his eyes straight forward, knowing that the four airmen were there beside him.

The swell of the music let him know that the ceremony was over. The recessional was just the opposite of the march to the altar.

Now the bride and groom went first and the best man and ushers followed in reverse order. Now Chris would be the last. Ken was directly in front of him. He could hardly contain himself, he was so proud. He gave his arm to Penny without even looking at her. He didn't think of Laurie, either. He thought of nothing except the fact that he was walking literally in Ken's footsteps—Ken who might be an astronaut.

He saw Mom and looked at her, expecting her to be lost in admiration of the airmen. She had eyes only for Chris.

"Oh, Mom," he whispered to himself.

At the reception he was delighted when Jack said to him, "Come on, Chris, we're at the bride's table."

"All of us?" Chris asked.

"Yeah, the whole wedding party."

Chris just couldn't believe his good fortune. He'd be at the table with Ken. Maybe he could talk to him about Edwards Air Force Base, and about his astronaut training. Maybe—Chris felt himself going shy at the thought—but maybe he could confide to Ken his dream of one day going to the moon.

But Chris wasn't at the table very long before he realized that Ken had other ideas. Maybe he was going to take astronaut training, maybe he was going to the moon some day, but right now he was here strictly for the wedding, and he apparently was enjoying himself every minute.

Jack turned around. "Say, isn't that music ever going to start?"

"Why?" Chris asked.

"For the dancing, fella. For the dancing."

"Are you going to dance?"

"Am I going to dance? Why do you think I came all the way up here for the wedding? Sure I'm going to dance."

"Is Ken going to dance?" Chris asked, hoping for an answer in the negative. Maybe they could sit and talk while the others danced.

"Is Ken going to dance! Just about the best old dancer in the air force, that's what Ken is. How do you think he's going to go rolling around in outer space if he doesn't know how to dance?"

"Can you dance, fella?" Jack asked.

"No," Chris answered. For a fleeting second Chris almost wished that he could dance, but only for a second. Then he thought of M.T. and their blood-brotherly vow never to dance.

"No, I can't dance," he repeated firmly.

Jack was undisturbed by his emphasis. "Do you know what I'm going to do?" he asked. "I'm going to have the first dance with the bridesmaid I escorted. Then I'm going to dance with that pretty mother of yours."

"Well, she can dance!" Chris said proudly.

Chris sat watching the airmen as they danced, especially Ken. Jack was right. Ken certainly knew how to dance. Then a horrible thought struck him. He remembered Jack's words, "How do you think he's going to go rolling around in outer space if he doesn't know how to dance?" Suppose that was a requirement for going into outer space.

Chris held the thought for one miserable second, then relegated it to the back of his mind—his storehouse for unpleasant thoughts.

Well, nothing was going to keep him from the moon! He was sure of that.

All the way home from the wedding Chris regaled Mom with tales of Bob and Bill, Jack and Ken, but mostly Ken, who might be an astronaut.

As he went into his room, weary but happy, he noticed a new pair of pajamas folded on the bed. On a blue background were large yellow prints of moons, planets and stars. Down the front were a double row of buttons in the shape of missiles.

"Gosh, Mom," Chris said.

"Just a little reward, Chris. I bought them a few days ago. After all, you did go through quite a bit for the wedding."

He hurried to his room and changed his wedding uniform for his astronaut pajamas. He'd certainly like M.T. to see them. He was sure M.T. would say, "Sharpo. Double sharpo."

He popped into the kitchen where Mom was just making hot chocolate.

"They sure are sharp, Mom. I sure like them." Then he added honestly, "But you didn't have to buy them. I don't need a reward. The wedding turned out to be real super, Mom."

She ran her hand through his little stubble of hair. "Are you growing up, my Chris?"

"I don't know, Mom, am I?"

He thought again of the airmen he had met at the wedding. "You sure can dance, Mom. Jack said so, and so did Ken who might be . . ."

"An astronaut," she finished for him.

Then she gave him one of her teasing looks. "I'm going to have a dance with you some day, moon man," she said.

12: "Everything Happens to Me"

On Monday morning Chris saw Mr. Lawrence in the yard before school.

"Well, Astro," Mr. Lawrence said, "you seem to have survived the wedding."

"Oh, Mr. Lawrence, I met a real live astronaut at the wedding. At least he's at the Edwards Air Force Training Base for astronauts." Chris went on excitedly, "All the ushers were airmen. Except me, of course."

"And you're a moon man at heart." Mr. Lawrence laughed. "See, Chris, I told you. You meet the most interesting people at weddings. I have some exciting news to tell you at practice today, too."

"Oh, what is it, Mr. Lawrence? Please tell me now."

"I can't Astro. I have to tell everyone at the same time."

Chris really had an exciting morning. With trying to give M.T. little asides about the astronauts at the wedding, and anticipating what Mr. Lawrence was going to tell at practice, Chris' lessons were a little slighted.

He told M.T. what Mr. Lawrence had said. M.T. evidently told someone, and that one told another, so Mr. Lawrence met a very enthusiastic group in the gym for the accelerated practice.

"Well, this is it, fellows: we play Polk School a week from Wednesday and then a game each week until we are eliminated. And I hope we are not eliminated. I hope that Westcliff goes all the way."

Mr. Lawrence's words were greeted with cheers and clapping.

"All right now!" Mr. Lawrence fairly shouted. "Let's have a little of that enthusiasm here on the court."

They had the best practice they'd ever had.

At the end of the game, Mr. Lawrence said, "Wait a minute, Doc and Astro."

Mr. Lawrence pushed his hands into his pockets and rocked back on his heels. He smiled a warm approval. "If you two keep up the kind of work you gave us today, no elementary-school team can stop us. I'm sure of that."

Chris and M.T. walked home together enjoying the ultimate in friendship, where neither said a word because he was too full of joy even to utter one, but not having to because he knew that his friend would understand.

Later Chris sat opposite Mom at the dinner table in a complete whirl of thought. He was recalling his short but exciting association with the airmen, he was still glowing at Mr. Lawrence's praise, and he could hardly contain himself at the thought of the coming game with Polk School.

"Mom," he blurted out, "we play Polk School, our first game, a week from Wednesday."

"Do you play during school time, Chris?"

"Gosh, no, Mom. This is strictly after-school athletics. I can just see Mrs. Johnstone letting us play another team during school time."

"But, Chris"—her surprise showing in her voice —"isn't a week from Wednesday the day of the competitive test at the lab?"

Chris felt as if he had been hit in the face with a shock of ice-cold water.

"It is, Mom. How could they possibly schedule the game for that day?"

"Well, it may be this way, Chris. You are the only one on the team from Westcliff who goes to the special lab. Maybe there are only a few or even none from Polk."

"But, Mom—" he started. Then stopped. He could hardly say that Mr. Lawrence considered him and

M.T. the very best players on the team. He knew how little his mother understood about basketball. To her it was just a game. It might as well have been tiddley winks that he and M.T. played on the floor when they were little.

He'd speak to Mr. Lawrence in the morning, but before he did he had a restless night to get through. He tossed and turned and slept fitfully. Every time he awakened he was conscious of the light in Mr. Kitchenger's house. His nephew must still be working on his western area maps. Chris squirmed uneasily when he remembered how he had thought the nephew was a threat to Edwards Air Force Base. Then his sleepy thoughts turned to Ken and the astronaut training at Edwards. On this happy thought he fell asleep, and stayed asleep until Mom called him in the morning.

Chris didn't see Mr. Lawrence before school, but he had planned anyhow to go to his room at twelve-thirty for a private talk.

"You're right, Astro," Mr. Lawrence said in emphatic surprise. "I suppose no one even thought of the after-school lab sessions when the games were scheduled."

"What are we doing to do, Mr. Lawrence?"

"There's nothing we can do. You were especially selected to go to the science laboratory, Chris. Your duty lies there. You'll just have to miss the first game, that's all."

That's all! Chris never quite knew how he left Mr. Lawrence's room and reached his own classroom, and how he went through the remainder of the day.

He left school immediately at dismissal. Mr. Lawrence hadn't said, but he assumed that since the practice was for the Polk game he wouldn't be needed.

He walked slowly along, his mind seething, and though no one could make him admit it, an aching feeling in his heart.

This was a time a fellow would like to talk to his dad.

He wandered aimlessly around his room until dinner time. He thought he was acting as if nothing had happened, but it was pretty hard to fool Mom.

"What is it, Chris?" she asked.

Then he told her the whole thing.

"But Mr. Lawrence was right, Chris. He couldn't change the schedule. That must be a school department setup. And your first commitment *is* to the lab."

"But why does everything have to happen to me?

Even Mr. Kitchenger. He hates me. I can't even walk in front of his house."

"Probably so many things happen to you, because you are in so many things. M.T. is on the team; Percy goes to the lab; but you do both, Chris. And Mr. Kitchenger really doesn't hate you. He's just annoyed at the boy next door. If Percy lived here, Mr. Kitchenger would be annoyed at him."

"Well, I wish Percy did live here."

"I don't. I'd much rather have you living here with me."

"Gosh, Mom." Chris laughed with her.

The laugh helped, and he decided he wouldn't say anything about his real great hurt—the fact that though he knew Mr. Lawrence considered him and M.T. his best players, he let him out of the Polk game without even saying he'd miss him.

The first thing in the morning Mr. Lawrence sent for him and asked why he had missed practice.

"I thought the practice was for the Polk game, and since..."

"The practice is for all the games. Be there this afternoon and every afternoon."

Chris was there and played his heart out every afternoon. On Tuesday, before the Polk game, as Chris was on his way to the lockers after practice,

Mr. Lawrence gave him an affectionate slap that stung right through his basketball trunks.

"We'll certainly miss you at the game tomorrow, Astro."

Gosh. Gosh.

Chris' happiness carried him through the rest of the evening, through the next day, and through the competitive test at the lab. He knew he did well. He felt that he was on the tiptop of the world. As he turned in his test paper, he looked at Percy. Percy was lost in thought, his brows furrowed, slowly chewing the top of his ball-point pen.

Chris felt good all over. On his way out he passed through the hall where the projects were on display.

Today was the last lab session for the term, and he knew that the projects would not be returned until after the awards were made.

He decided to take a quick look at them again. His and Percy's were side by side. Percy's was a model of efficiency and neatness. Even the card bearing his name and title of the project was lettered and mounted perfectly.

Old Percy! Chris was sure that he also would be in to take one last look at the project.

Suddenly touched by his gay impulsiveness, Chris quickly changed the name cards on the two exhibits. Then he jumped behind a pole. Wait until

Percy saw that! Chris was already laughing in anticipation of the look on Percy's face. Wait until he jumped out from behind the pole and teased Percy about the changed cards.

But Chris waited and waited, and still Percy didn't come. Chris knew how meticulous Percy was, and how he was probably going over every question about five times. Finally Chris decided that he had been waiting overly long and thought he'd better go back to the classroom and check.

Just as he reached the classroom, he saw Percy leaving the building by the side entrance.

"Hey, Percy, wait, wait!" Chris caught up with him and the two of them walked along and discussed the test. Chris felt confident, but as usual, Percy was deeply worried. Percy always fretted about tests and then usually came out with an A.

They walked along, Chris happy, Percy still worried, and Chris in a great hurry to see M.T. and find the outcome of the Polk game.

Any thought of the switched cards on the laboratory projects had completely slipped his mind.

13: The Winner

Westcliff School was the victor in the Polk game and then went on week after week to be the winning team in the elementary-school basketball league. In each game Chris and M.T. became more proficient and more and more popular.

On the other hand Percy grew more restless as each week passed, and he kept bothering Chris about news of the lab award.

"You know all awards are made close to the end of the term," Chris explained.

"I know, but I feel that the laboratory award is different. The lab is already closed for the term, so why not give the award now?"

"Cheer up, Percy. The time is almost here. Just another week. You know the rules of the contest. The award will be presented at an assembly at the school of the winner."

"Do you think the winner won't know until that very day?"

"I'm sure the school will have to know a day or so before, so perhaps the winner will, too."

"Well, it's so long to wait," Percy complained.

But the waiting hadn't been hard for Chris. His mind was so taken up with the basketball series. True, every time he saw Percy he thought of the lab competition, and often he thought of it when he was in bed at night. Mom spoke of it, too (hopefully, he thought), and he never came in contact with Mrs. Johnstone that she didn't say, "I certainly hope the laboratory award is coming to Westcliff."

But the day of the game with Northgate all thought of the laboratory award was crowded out of Chris' mind. Westcliff, with Chris and M.T. in starring roles, decisively defeated the opponent team.

Mr. Lawrence jumped as high as the basketball standards. "Here we come, Southcliff!" he shouted. "Fellows, next week we play the pennant game. We have to win. We just have to."

Chris walked home with no thought at all except the one concerning the coming game with Southcliff. Even the sight of Percy put no other idea into his mind.

"Chris, Chris, wait," Percy called as he hurried to catch up with him. "The award assembly should be in two more days. Do you suppose anyone has heard yet?"

"Heard what?"

"Heard what!" As if he had been struck, Percy stopped and looked searchingly at Chris.

Chris laughed as he suddenly realized what Percy was talking about. "Oh, the lab award. Gosh, Percy, I forgot all about it."

"You forgot all about it?" Percy's eyes were almost as large as the horn-rimmed glasses that covered them.

Chris put his arm around Percy's shoulder. "Percy, I've been so busy with the basketball series. We beat Northgate today." He gave Percy an emphasizing shove that almost knocked him over. "Do you realize that now we play Southcliff for the pennant next week?"

"Is that so?" Percy asked, displaying not the slightest interest.

"Cheer up, Percy. The game is next Wednesday, but the award assembly will take place before that. Good luck."

Chris meant it sincerely. Poor Perc. After all, he didn't have basketball, and Chris was sure he didn't have any aspirations of going to the moon either.

Chris continued his homeward trip of a skip and a hop and a jump. He was sure Mom would be happy about the game. True, she didn't understand much about basketball, and he never really tried to explain the rules to her, but he knew she would be happy to know that Westcliff was going all the way. He knew, too, that she realized the importance of the series because Mr. Lawrence hadn't had time for weeks to indulge in one of her nourishing meals.

Mom's meals! He certainly was hungry. A boy certainly worked up an appetite in a basketball game. He knew that Mom would have dinner ready as soon as he arrived home. He broke into a run.

When he reached his house a man was standing on the steps talking to a boy from across the street.

"Here's Chris now," the boy said.

"Are you Chris Muldoon?"

"Yes," Chris answered.

"Hurry, then. We've been waiting for you."

When Chris walked into the house, he was bewildered. The living room was crowded. There were men with cameras, and men with note pads.

"Oh, Chris! Chris!" Mom said as she put her arms around him.

"Hold it, Mrs. Muldoon, hold it."

Chris turned just as a light bulb flashed in his eyes.

"Now it's spoiled," the man said. "We'll have to do another one. Here, let's pose it now."

"Mom," Chris asked, "what's the matter?"

"All right now, all right," the camera man said. "Just look here. Come on, both of you, give us a big smile."

Chris quickly did as he was told. He wanted to get it over with and find out what was going on.

"Mom?" he started, but someone rushed from the sofa and caught his hand.

"Oh, Chris! Chris, we are all so proud of you. You have brought honor to Westcliff School."

Chris almost fainted. It was Mrs. Johnstone.

"Here, let's get a picture of him with the principal."

Someone pushed him. "Here, Mrs. Johnstone, put your arm around him please."

Mrs. Johnstone responded with alacrity. Chris stood as if he was frozen to the spot.

"Smile. Smile. Thank you, Mrs. Johnstone. That's wonderful. Come on now, Chris. Smile."

Chris couldn't. He simply couldn't.

The bulbs flashed and the ordeal was over.

"Now one of him alone."

Chris, in his stunned surprise and bewilderment, tried to figure things out. It was rather silly to take pictures now. Why didn't they wait until after the Southcliff game? That was the game which would tell. Why were they taking pictures of him? M.T. had been just as good. Well, maybe they were going to M.T.'s house next. But then, why Mrs. Johnstone instead of Mr. Lawrence? He was the coach.

Finally Chris' tongue loosened. "Why did you come here?" he asked the nearest photographer.

"Why didn't you come to the game where Mr. Lawrence and all of us were?"

"What game?" the photographer asked.

"The one with Northgate." Now that Chris had started to talk he went right on, "and besides I don't know why you didn't wait until we play Southcliff next week. That's the pennant game."

Mrs. Johnstone came forward, understanding in her eyes. "Chris, all this excitement has nothing to do with the game. We are all here about the laboratory award. You are the winner. Percy is the runner-up. Just think, both from Westcliff School. Oh, I am so proud.

"School hadn't been dismissed for ten minutes when the reporters and photographers came asking for you. Miss Foster told them you were at the game. They decided to come here rather than go to the game. They insisted that I come, too."

Chris just stared at her. She was Mrs. Johnstone all right, but he had never heard her talk like that, especially to him.

"Yes, Mrs. Johnstone," he said blankly.

Mrs. Johnstone turned to the photographers. "Are you planning to take a picture of the runner-up?"

"Say that wouldn't be a bad idea."

So there was a general flurry of exits. The photographers were gathering their equipment, the reporters were stuffing notes into pockets, Mom was pushing Chris toward Mrs. Johnstone, insisting on a polite good-bye. Chris moved through the whole thing as if he were in a daze.

Finally all were gone. He and Mom were alone. She put her arms around him and held him tight.

"Chris, Chris, I'm so proud of you."

"Gosh, Mom, gosh."

14: Award Assembly

Mom called to Chris while he was in the shower. "Chris, I've put your things out on the bed—your slacks, white shirt and jacket."

"What did you say, Mom?" Chris asked above the splashing of the water.

She repeated, but much louder this time.

Quickly Chris turned off the water, encased himself in a huge towel, stepped onto the tile of the bathroom floor, his feet dripping wet, the water making little riverlets all down his surprised-looking face.

"Why all the fancy stuff, Mom? I'm just going to school."

"Christopher Muldoon, don't tell me that you have forgotten that today is the award assembly."

"Gosh, Mom. Guess I'm not quite wide awake yet."

"Really, Chris, if I wasn't your own mother I might wonder how you remembered the answers long enough to pass that test."

But when she bade him good-bye as he left for school, he knew she wasn't really annoyed. Her cheeks were pink and pretty, and he knew that she was excited.

"I'll see you at the assembly. Don't be nervous now."

Nervous? Then Chris realized that the auditorium would be crowded. There would be all the upper-grade pupils of Westcliff, the special students from the lab, their parents and friends. He and Percy would have to be on stage, he realized.

When, at eleven o'clock, the bell rang for assembly, Chris saw that he had been right. The auditorium was crowded, and he and Percy were to sit on the stage.

Chris saw Mom as he walked up the aisle. If only Dad could be here, too.

Miss Foster was beaming.

"Atta boy, Astro," Mr. Lawrence said softly as Chris passed him on the way to the stage.

Chris took his place on the stage at the right side of Mrs. Johnstone. Percy was at the left. The lab superintendent and his assistant sat across from them.

The superintendent gave a speech about the lab, its facilities and purposes. He told about the competitive test, and about the medal he was now going to award.

"Will Christopher Muldoon please come forward?"

Chris' knees shook a little as he walked to the front of the stage. He could see Mom. She looked so happy. So did Miss Foster. Mr. Lawrence gave him a little victory sign.

The assistant walked to the superintendent, holding the open box which contained the medal.

Dramatically the superintendent took the medal, pinned it on Chris' lapel as he said, "Christopher Muldoon, I award you this medal for scientific achievement."

"Thank you," Chris managed to murmur as the superintendent shook his hand.

The superintendent had barely let go the hand when Mrs. Johnstone was there shaking hands with Chris.

"Congratulations, Chris," she said in a voice that could be heard all over the auditorium, "and thank you for bringing honor to Westcliff School."

Somehow Chris stumbled back to his place and sat there with a mixture of emotions. He was thrilled with the medal. He was delighted for Mom. If only Dad were here. It was a little embarrassing on the stage facing everyone. He could see Laurie sitting on the aisle. She kept trying to wave to him.

He looked at Percy being handed his award. He wondered how he felt. Chris' wandering attention focused long enough to realize that Percy wasn't re-

ceiving a medal. The superintendent was handing him a large certificate. What was he saying? Now Chris listened intently.

"This is the first year a runner-up award has been given," the superintendent said. He chuckled a little and went on, "in fact this is the first time, and the only time this situation has occurred. A really unusual situation indeed," he mused quite aloud. "For the first time in the history of the competition, both boys had exactly the same score on their test papers."

Then evidently sensing the stirred interest of the audience, he held up his hand. "What did we do? Ah, we had a way to take care of that."

Chris bent forward on his chair. He could see Percy staring.

"You see," the superintendent went on, taking the whole audience into his confidence, "each student at the laboratory had an individual term project. The projects were finished, each one complete with name plate. So we used these projects to break the tie. The projects were examined minutely, and since Christopher Muldoon had the far better project, he became the winner, and so we thought it only right to give Percival a runner-up award."

Chris was on his feet shouting, "No! No! No!"

Mrs. Johnstone pulled at his arm. "Chris, Chris, what in the world is the matter? Sit down. Sit down!"

"It's not mine. It's not mine." Chris was so upset his fingers fumbled as he tried to get the pin off his lapel.

He ran forward on the stage, pressed the pin into the superintendent's hand. "There was a mistake. I changed the name plates. The winning project was Percy's."

Blindly he ran down the side steps of the stage, along the middle aisle and out of the auditorium. As he ran someone sitting on the aisle caught his hand and whispered, "Oh, Chris, Chris." Later he realized that it was Laurie.

But he paid no attention then. He kept right on running, out to the sidewalk, along the street until he reached the sands of the beach.

He threw himself on his back and lay staring at the sky, spent and exhausted from the shock and disgrace of the morning.

Why in the world had he changed those name plates? He had just done it for a lark, and it seemed such fun at the time. Again he saw himself hiding behind the pole at the lab waiting to see the expression on Percy's face. If only Percy had come along then, instead of going out the other door. But why in all these weeks had he never given the name plates another thought? Why hadn't he thought of it when he heard he was the winner? True, he hadn't any idea that the projects were going to be considered in the competition. Nobody had. In fact the superintendent had reveled in the surprise of his announcement. But even so, why had he forgotten?

Then as clearly as if she were standing there at the minute he heard his mother's words, "Impulsive and forgetful, and they are going to get you into trouble if you aren't careful."

Well, they certainly did get him into trouble, the worst he could possibly think of, and now Mom was innocently involved. She had been so proud of their pictures in yesterday's paper. What would tomorrow's paper say?

And what of M.T., and Percy, and Laurie? It was then he remembered the hand that had caught at his as he ran from the auditorium. It was Laurie's, he realized, held out in comfort.

But what of Mr. Lawrence? Chris sat up straight, dug his fingers again into the warm sand, and looked unseeingly out to the horizon. Yes, what about Mr. Lawrence? Next to Dad's, Chris valued Mr. Lawrence's opinion. Well, he'd know about Mr. Lawrence in the morning.

But Mom! Mom!

Now he was on his feet, his heart racing, his tongue dry in his mouth. What had he done to her? How could he possibly face her? But he'd have to, and right now.

He started home, but his feet dragged. How would she be? he wondered. Would there be the staccato heel, the staccato tones of her voice, and the round pink spots on her cheeks?

Would she say the minute she saw him, "Impulsive and forgetful? I always said they would get into trouble some day. And now they have. You have not only embarrassed me before the neighborhood, you have embarrassed me before the whole city. How am I ever going to face anyone again?"

But there was none of this; no staccato tones, no pink cheeks, no words of recrimination.

His mother was in the kitchen preparing dinner. She looked white and drained. She said only one thing. "Chris, I'm glad your father wasn't there today."

15: Aftermath

M.T. met Chris at the corner the next morning and gave him the old hand clasp. "Gosh, Chris, I'm sorry. I wanted to go to your house last night or call you, but I was afraid your mother wouldn't like it."

"That's the worst part—Mom."

"Is she really giving it to you?"

Chris shook his head. "No. That's it. She hardly said anything."

M.T. walked with him in mute sympathy. Just as they turned the corner he shoved Chris into a doorway. "Golly, there's Percy. I'm sure you don't want to meet him now."

"I wish I didn't have to meet him ever, but I do. May as well be now."

M.T. evidently decided to act as an emissary. "Hey, Percy. Wait."

Chris had read stories of men walking the plank, and now the full meaning of the tales came to him. He thought he knew exactly how they felt. He moistened his lips, but simply could not force the words from his mouth. To his amazement Percy took care of that.

"Chris, why in the world did you go dashing off the stage? The superintendent gave me the medal that you thrust into his hands, but the certificate belongs to you. Of course, the name will have to be changed."

Now, more than ever, Chris couldn't speak. He was conscious of M.T. standing with his mouth open and his quarter inch of blond hair more bristling than ever. Percy wasn't even angry.

"It was very careless of them to mix up those projects."

"I changed the cards, Percy. Didn't you hear me say so when I shoved the medal into the superintendent's hand?"

"You changed the cards?"

"Yes, and that is what caused the . . . the . . ."

M.T. of the large vocabulary supplied the word, "fiasco."

Even in his misery Chris couldn't help giving a tiny smile. The way M.T. talked!

"I changed the cards on the projects and hid behind the pole at the laboratory waiting to see the look on your face. Then you went out the back way. I followed you, and never gave it another thought until I heard the superintendent speaking."

Chris braced himself for Percy's reply. After all, he, Chris, had caused whatever it was M.T. called it, and he had cheated Percy of the honor of receiving the medal first-hand. Chris could feel M.T. standing shoulder to shoulder with him in blood-brother support.

"You played a joke on me like you always play jokes on M.T.?"

Chris stood dumb, trying to turn away from the friendship-hungry look on Percy's face.

But now M.T. was completely in charge of the situation. Putting an arm around each boy's shoulder he said, "Come on, Chris; come on, Perc, if we don't hurry we'll be late and then we'll all be in trouble."

Chris heard Percy give a chuckle of delight, probably at the thought of being included in the companionable trouble.

They reached school just in time to avoid being late, but not in time for Chris to avoid being in trouble.

The minute he put his foot into the hall, he saw Mrs. Johnstone standing at the door of her office.

"Chris Muldoon," she called out when he was within a few feet of her, "I'll see you in my office immediately."

He followed her into the room. She took her place at the desk and sat there straight and tall. Her lips were a thin line, and her eyes seemed to pierce right through him.

"I hope you realize, Chris Muldoon, that you have brought dishonor and disgrace to Westcliff School." She went on with a torrent of words, sterner and more severe than he had ever heard her.

Chris' mind was too numb for the whole meaning to register, but he clearly understood her when she said, "I will not tolerate cheating at Westcliff."

"Cheating?" Chris was staggered into speech.

"Be still, Chris Muldoon," she went on. "You turned the whole assembly into a shambles. Before all our visitors you shouted out and then dashed from the auditorium causing more disgrace."

Suddenly she sat back in her chair. "Now what do you have to say for yourself, Chris Muldoon?"

"Mrs. Johnstone, I wasn't cheating."

"What do you call taking someone's project for your own?"

Chris tried and tried to explain, but the more he tried, the more he realized that it would be difficult to make others understand that it was only an impulsive act.

He gave up trying and was relieved to hear Mrs. Johnstone say, "Return to your classroom. I'll see you later."

Then she stopped him as he reached the door. "No," she said, "we may as well take care of the matter now. Before you go to your classroom, stop at Mr. Lawrence's room and tell him that you are not to be in the Southcliff game."

"Mrs. Johnstone, that is the pennant game."

"Then, to be more specific," Mrs. Johnstone said emphatically, "you are not to be in the pennant game."

Chris walked down the hall, one huge ache. Not to be in the Southcliff game! And Mr. Lawrence? What would Mr. Lawrence say?

Chris knocked on the classroom door, and Mr. Lawrence came out and stood in the hall. He waited for Chris to speak.

"Mr. Lawrence," Chris blurted out, "Mrs. Johnstone says that I am not to be in the Southcliff game."

"That's a fair punishment," Mr. Lawrence replied. There was no inflection in his voice, no expression on his face.

"Mr. Lawrence, Mrs. Johnstone thinks I was cheating. I wasn't, Mr. Lawrence." Chris went on to explain his silly prank at lab, and how he had completely forgotten it until the superintendent mentioned the project.

Mr. Lawrence just listened without changing expression or saying a word.

Chris shifted from one foot to the other, then lamely said, "Mr. Lawrence, I think I'd better go to my class room."

"Yes, I think you had."

Chris didn't know where to turn, what to do. He went to his classroom and tried to pay attention to his lesson, but he really didn't know what was going on. Then just before recess he made his decision. He would talk to Miss Foster.

When the other boys and girls went out he stayed in the room. "Miss Foster, may I talk to you a minute?"

"Of course, Chris," she said.

"Miss Foster," he started, and hesitated. Then he went on with a torrent of words as rapid as Mrs. Johnstone's had been. He explained about his silly prank at the lab, about Mrs. Johnstone, about Mr. Lawrence. He paused briefly for breath and for courage. Strange. This was the way he would ordinarily talk to Mr. Lawrence and not to Miss Foster.

"Miss Foster, do you think I intended to cheat?"

She didn't hesitate even a split second. "No, Chris. I didn't know what silly nonsense you were up to this time, but I knew it was nothing dishonest."

"Thank you, Miss Foster."

"I know you like a book, Chris." She smiled at him. "And it's a book I rather like."

Chris waited a few seconds. "Miss Foster, I brought my lunch today, but I'd like to go home at noon to see Mom. I want to be sure she knows I wasn't cheating."

"Chris, I'm positive she knows you weren't cheating. But I do think it would be a good idea for you to go home at noon today. Chris, you have a great deal to make up to your mother. You must have hurt her very much."

"I know, Miss Foster. I wish I knew how to make it up to her."

Miss Foster smiled at him. "It will have to be many, many little things, Chris. Don't go out and try some spectacular and stir things up again. Just little things."

Her eyes twinkled as she looked right at him. "Just little things—such as being a wonderful Columbus in our play, and making your mother proud, instead of wishing to be a space man in Mr. Lawrence's play."

Chris stared at her in astonishment. "Miss Foster, how did you know?"

"I've been teaching a long time, Chris." She laughed softly, and started toward the door. "I'll go to Mrs. Johnstone to see if I can get a pass for you."

Chris didn't know what happened in the office, but he was given the pass and went home at noon, lunch box in hand, to see Mom.

She was just sitting down to have her own lunch.

"Don't bother about me, Mom. I brought my lunch with me."

He opened his box and ate the lunch that he would have eaten at school. The whole time he kept talking to Mom, explaining, explaining.

She didn't say much but Chris could see understanding in her eyes.

"Mom, it was what you always said about me, *Impulsive and forgetful.* Mom, if you'll forgive me this time, I promise never to be impulsive or forgetful again."

Mom gave him a searching look. Just then the hall clock chimed the three-quarters of the hour.

She said hurriedly, "Chris, from what you tell me, your status with Mrs. Johnstone is not the very best right now. You'd better not be late."

"That's right." Chris jumped up. "'Bye, Mom," he said as he grabbed his lunch box and ran for the door.

"Chris," she called after him, "why are you taking your lunch box? It's empty."

"Oh, Mom, I forgot."

Quickly Mom lowered her eyes, but not before Chris saw a twinkle in them. Soft pink touched the cheeks that had been so paper-white since yesterday.

Impulsively Chris put his arms around her. "Gosh, Mom, gosh."

16: A Rescue

The week-end had been good for Chris. There were no explanations to make, and Mom had been kind and generous.

Now it was Monday morning and Chris had another problem. What about basketball practice? There were only two days before the pennant game. Surely if he wasn't going to be in the game there was no need for him to practice. Still, the last time, Mr. Lawrence had expected him. Chris dreaded the thought of going to practice and being dismissed in front of everyone, but even more, though, he dreaded the idea of confronting Mr. Lawrence alone.

Finally he decided on the latter idea. At the noon recess he knocked timidly on Mr. Lawrence's door.

"Come in," Mr. Lawrence called. He was seated at his desk correcting papers when Chris went in.

"What is it, Muldoon?" he asked, still making red marks on the papers.

The name *Muldoon* let Chris know immediately how the situation lay. No *Astro;* not even *Chris.*

Chris shuffled uneasily and struggled to get the

144

words out. "Mr. Lawrence, I wasn't sure about practice today and tomorrow."

"No need." Mr. Lawrence clipped his words. "You're out of the game; so why practice?"

"Yes, Mr. Lawrence," Chris mumbled and started for the door.

When he was halfway there, Mr. Lawrence's words stopped him. "Muldoon, no one is ever going to the moon unless he first has his feet on the ground. Anyone who is as unresponsible as you were at the lab would forget to fire his re-entry rockets."

Somehow Chris reached the door and left the room, but his misery must have shown plainly on his face. When he met Miss Foster in the hall a few minutes later, she remarked, "I see the going is still rough, Chris. But remember what I told you about the little things. You'll have to make it up to Mr. Lawrence as well as your mother. He's so disappointed because he's your friend as well as your coach."

"Yes, Miss Foster," Chris mumbled.

"Be in the stands Wednesday and cheer Westcliff to victory." She put her hand on his shoulder. "Remember, little things."

Late that night Chris remembered what she had said about spectaculars, and about little things.

Following an unhappy after-school period dribbling the basketball up and down his own back yard, accompanied by Mr. Kitchenger's chant, "Be sure you keep that ball in your yard, Chris Muldoon," a quiet dinner with Mom, Chris went to his own room as soon as he reasonably could.

He sat on the floor, his arms on the window ledge, gazing unseeingly at the house next door. Then suddenly he realized that Mr. Kitchenger's nephew must have gone. The Monza hadn't been outside all week-end, and it wasn't there now either. Now that Chris thought of it, for several nights there hadn't been a light in the room that the nephew used.

Chris had to laugh as he thought of something else. All the time that the nephew was there, there was no yelling from Mr. Kitchenger. Well, the nephew must have gone. Mr. Kitchenger had certainly been in top form as Chris dribbled the ball up and down the yard this afternoon.

Chris decided that he might as well go to bed, but once there he tossed and turned uncomfortably. He couldn't forget Mr. Lawrence's words about the moon flight. Then he thought of Miss Foster. How many little things would it take to make Mr. Lawrence call him *Astro* again? And what kind of little things?

"Little things, little things," he repeated over and over, becoming drowsy with the sameness of the chant. He squirmed to get more comfortable in bed. Half asleep, he noticed a glow on the wall. Probably a reflection from the sky. How long it was since he used to scan the sky at night.

Suddenly he was wide awake! The whole room was lighted by the glow. In a second he was at the window.

Mr. Kitchenger's house was on fire!

Almost automatically Chris grabbed for his rope ladder. He was not even conscious of the stinging of the rope on his bare feet. Even more quickly than on the night he drew Mr. Kitchenger's ire, he was down the ladder and across the short distance to the old man's house. It was a good thing the house was an exact duplicate of his own. He would know how to find his way around.

He knew that the one window that was open was in the bathroom. The fire had not reached there yet. Good. The drainpipe was right outside. Quickly he climbed, and crawled up the pipe, all the time trying to recall all the safety measures the fireman had told them that day in the auditorium.

Then clearly he remembered the most important one: "Never forget, never forget—you are not a fireman. Call the fire department. Never mind the heroics."

He tried to slide down the pipe, but he had to

yank at his pajama top because a button had caught between the drainpipe and the house.

With his feet firmly on the ground, he knew it would be quicker to reach the fire-alarm box three doors from Mr. Kitchenger's house than it would be to scramble back into his own house and telephone.

He broke the glass and set off the alarm. The fireman had told them always to stand by the fire box to direct the firemen, but there was no need for this. The minute the engines turned the corner, the firemen would see Mr. Kitchenger's burning house.

Chris was sorely tempted. Here was his opportunity to replace the fiasco at the lab with real heroics. But just as surely as if she had been standing there Chris heard Miss Foster's words, "Not a spectacular; just little things, little things."

Quickly he ran from the fire box and used his rope ladder to go back into his room. He hardly had his feet on the floor when he heard his mother calling, "Chris. Chris."

"Mom, Mr. Kitchenger's house is on fire!" he shouted.

Quickly he put on his robe and slippers, and grabbing his coat, met Mom in the hall. She, too, was in slippers, robe and coat. They went outside to join the crowd that was growing larger by the minute.

Firemen were running, hoses had been dragged into position, the ambulance drove up, police were swarming around and efficient hands lifted Mr. Kitchenger into the ambulance.

As is usual in excited crowds watching a fire, truth and untruth were equally passed around as absolute fact.

Officer O'Looney came up to Mom the minute he saw her. "I knew you'd be worried, Mrs. Muldoon. Old Kitchenger was rescued. The firemen were there before the flames reached his side of the house. Somebody certainly turned the alarm right on the dot, but in all the confusion nobody seems to know who the hero is."

"The main thing is the fact that Mr. Kitchenger was saved, Officer O'Looney."

"That's right, Mrs. Muldoon. I hear that they took him to the hospital just to be sure, because of his age." Officer O'Looney scratched his head. "Still some hero is going around unnoticed."

Again Chris was sorely tempted. Suppose he let them know that he was the one who had turned in the alarm? How would Mom feel? Would she be proud of him? And Mr. Lawrence? Would he think that Chris really had his feet on the ground now?

But then again the words, "little things, little

things," echoed in his mind. Chris stood quietly at Mom's side.

When the fire was under control and the crowd began to dwindle, Officer O'Looney came back. "It's safe to go into your house now, Mrs. Muldoon. And don't be afraid. Firemen will be on duty all night."

"I'll make some hot chocolate," Mom said as soon as they reached the kitchen.

Chris went into his room to remove his coat and took off his robe, too.

As he sat across the table from Mom she said, "Chris, you've lost a button off your pajamas."

"I have?" he questioned in surprise, reaching for the missile-like buttons on his astronaut pajamas.

He ran his hand along his pajama jacket to see where the button was missing, but before he had even located the spot Mom called in shocked surprise, "Chris Muldoon, look at those hands. Don't tell me you went to bed with such dirty hands. They are positively black. Go into the bathroom this minute and wash them before you even touch that cup."

Chris was glad to retreat into the bathroom before Mom asked him any more questions. He did such a good job on his hands that Mom finally called out, "Chris, do you want your chocolate to get cold?"

When he finished his chocolate and went to bed he was really weary from all the exciting events of the night. He fought off sleep long enough to wonder again what Mom would think if she really knew. And Mr. Lawrence. Would he call him *Astro* again?

He would tell M.T., though. He would tell him the first thing in the morning. M.T. would love the secrecy, and the idea of the unknown hero.

Hero! And for saving Mr. Kitchenger, of all people!

Chris certainly didn't feel anything like a hero on the day of the pennant game. He tried to slide into the stands unnoticed, but he knew that everyone was conscious he was there and why. Eyes turned away from him in embarrassment, and that was almost worse than being stared at. Even the stir caused by the arrival of Mrs. Johnstone, who never attended the games, was only a fleeting one.

Mrs. Johnstone's presence in the stands gave the final stamp to the importance of this game. Westcliff had come all the way in their very first bid for the elementary-school championship, and today their hands were in clutching distance of that coveted pennant. The fact that Chris had played an important part in the series, and was now out of the final game was bitter fruit, indeed, to him. More bitter, still, was the knowledge that he was out by his own doing.

There was perfunctory clapping from the Westcliff stands, and wild shouting from the opposite stands as the Southcliff team came onto the floor.

Then things were reversed as the Westcliff team came out. Chris rose with the others and joined in the shouting and clapping as the Westcliff stands went wild.

Finally Mrs. Johnstone clapped her hands loudly demanding order as she had done many times in the schoolyard and school auditorium.

The Westcliff stands settled down. Chris felt a pushing in his row, and there was Laurie squeezing in beside him.

"Hi, Chris," she said.

"Hi, Laurie," he answered gratefully.

"Chris," Laurie whispered, "Miss Foster said to tell you she's proud of you."

"Proud of me?"

"Yes. She says it takes fortitude for you to be here. I call it ..."

Chris clamped his hand over her mouth. "Never mind. Never mind."

Then they laughed together. Good old Laurie. Suddenly he remembered himself and M.T. chasing a squealing Laurie to the water's edge when she was a little girl.

"Look, look!" Laurie's words broke into his train of thought. "M.T. is looking up into the stands. I know he's looking for you."

"He's not, Laurie."

"Yes, he is." Suddenly she was on her feet shouting, "M.T., M.T., here he is!"

M.T. looked up and held his hand toward Chris in the blood-brother grasp. Chris barely had time to return the salute when the whistle blew for the game to start.

M.T. and the center from Southcliff leaped for the ball. M.T. managed to tip it toward the Westcliff team. Westcliff took the lead and held it with a good safe margin, and M.T. was clearly the star of the game.

Westcliff entered the fourth quarter 70 to 60 with shouts and cheers of the Westcliff stands fairly raising the rafters. But within a few seconds of play the cheers were turned to moans because M.T. went down and had to be carried from the floor. In the time-out allowed for an injury, they learned that M.T.'s ankle had been twisted, not too badly, but enough to keep him out of the rest of the game.

The moans turned to quick conjecture. Who would take his place? Would M.T.'s absence take the spark from the Westcliff quintet? All eyes were on Mr. Lawrence. Who would be sent in?

Then Chris was startled by the sound of his own name being called out loudly and emphatically.

"Chris Muldoon!"

"Chris," Laurie said, "it's Mrs. Johnstone."

"Chris Muldoon," Mrs. Johnstone repeated. Her voice was as loud and clear as if it were coming over a loud speaker. "Chris," she said, not even moving from her place. "Chris, I know there is no time for you to get into one of those outfits now. Pull off your slip-over. I know all boys wear T-shirts. Get down there on the floor and take M.T.'s place. Somebody will give you a pair of Keds."

Chris sat stunned.

Laurie poked him in the ribs. "Go on, Chris. Go on. Do what Mrs. Johnstone says."

"But the coach makes the decisions."

"Yes, at every place but Westcliff."

"Chris Muldoon, do what I say immediately!" Mrs. Johnstone called out.

"Go on, Chris. Do what she says. Jump right down out of the stands."

Pushed and shoved by Laurie and aided by hands along the way, Chris crawled and slid and jumped and landed beside the players' bench and looked into Mr. Lawrence's uninviting eyes.

"All right," Mr. Lawrence said, his voice showing his reluctance, "this is not a college team, and Mrs. Johnstone is my principal, too, so let's do what she says. Come on, fellows, let's get him on the floor Hurry, our time-out is almost up."

Chris felt like a dummy being shunted from one to the other as many hands helped to roll up his trousers, pull off his sweater, untie his shoes.

"Here, I took M.T.'s Keds. I know they will fit you." Laurie was kneeling in front of him, putting the Keds on his feet.

"Laurie, how in the world did you get here?"

"The same way you did."

"You didn't jump out of the stands!"

"Of course, I did. Didn't you and M.T. teach me to climb fences and jump ditches?"

Just then Mr. Lawrence came toward them and Chris hoped he had a word of encouragement for him. But the teacher didn't even look at him. He spoke softly to Laurie. "You'd better just sit here on the players' bench. Evidently in all the excitement Mrs. Johnstone didn't see you jump out of the stands; but don't try to get back. And for goodness' sake, get something to cover that blond hair."

Just then the whistle blew and Chris went out to finish the last quarter without so much as a word from Mr. Lawrence.

The stands were wild with enthusiasm and encouragement, but Chris seemed unable to get anywhere, and neither did the forwards or the guards on the Westcliff team.

One field goal after another and a free throw sent

the Southcliff score soaring to 69, and time was running out.

Chris felt his heart a leaden thing in his chest. His team hadn't made a single point since he went in. He could hear the moans of the Westcliff stands and the pleading of Laurie and M.T., but not one word from Mr. Lawrence did he hear.

Then a personal foul was committed against Chris, and he knew he would have a chance from the free-throw line. If only he could make that one point. Then the score would be 71 to 69, and maybe Westcliff could hold on until the end. But if he missed, and Southcliff took the ball again they might have time for a field goal which would make the score Southcliff 71; Westcliff 70.

Oh, please. Please. If only he could get going. He went to the free-throw line knowing that when the ball was thrown onto the line he would have only ten seconds to get it into the basket.

A hush settled over the stands, and then he heard one voice, strong and pleading. "Astro, Astro, if ever you are going into orbit, make that moon shot now!"

Mr. Lawrence! Mr. Lawrence!

The ball was thrown on the free-throw line, and Chris grabbed it. Only ten seconds, but he took time to put his feet firmly on the ground first. Then as smoothly as he hoped to rise in his space capsule some day, he leaped into the air and sent the ball through the basket.

Westcliff 71 ; Southcliff 69.

A now-inspired Westcliff team kept their opponents from making another point. So the game ended with Westcliff the winner, and the pennant was theirs.

"Good," said Mrs. Johnstone loudly enough to be heard on the floor, and then left the gymnasium.

The players crowded around Chris, and the students in the stands sent down balloons and streamers and shouted Chris' name. But the real thrill came for Chris when Mr. Lawrence gave him the old affectionate swat and said, "Atta boy, Astro, atta boy."

18: A Man's Hand

Chris couldn't tell Mom about his part in the fire and she didn't understand much about basketball, although she was pleased to hear that Chris had given his best for Westcliff; but today he really had an opportunity to make her proud. Today the High Sixth grades would give their last assembly at Westcliff. Chris was determined to be the best Columbus who had ever played the part at the school. The performance would be something that his mother could see and understand.

And despite all his grumbling through the weeks of preparation and practice, he would be making no sacrifice in playing the part well. That is, after yesterday. What a surprise Miss Foster's class had received yesterday.

Each class had worked separately as usual, and they knew that by tradition the classes sat in the front of the auditorium as each teacher gave a talk. Then one class followed the other in presenting its play. As a climax the principal addressed the audience.

Yesterday when they came together for a general

rehearsal both classes were surprised, but Miss Foster's was completely delighted. Miss Foster, they learned, was to give a few introductory remarks to the parents, and Mr. Lawrence was to give the main speech.

Yesterday when the two classes met together, Mr. Lawrence outlined briefly what he was to say, but he told them enough that they realized he was tying the two plays together under one theme, and the title was *Spacemen All*.

Chris was ready now, but he couldn't find his Admiral's plume-adorned hat. When he had been fitted for his costume last week, the thought of wearing that hat outdid any of the horrors he had had about the wedding outfit. The airmen proved how wrong he had been about the wedding. Yesterday Mr. Lawrence had shown how wrong Chris was about the Admiral's hat. Today Chris would wear it proudly, that is, if he could find it.

He remembered seeing a large box in the corner of the hall just outside the dressing room. It had been filled with sailors' hats for the members of the crew. Maybe someone had put the Admiral's hat in the box.

In an instant Chris was bent over the box almost buried in a welter of sailors' hats. As he pushed hat after hat aside, looking for the plumed one, he became conscious of two people standing in the hall talking. He didn't know what to do. He didn't want to stand and interrupt them, but he didn't want to eavesdrop either. He went right on pushing hats aside, but he coughed loudly to let them know that someone was there. Evidently the sound of the cough was deadened by the hat-filled box.

"There's nothing to be nervous about," Miss Foster was saying. "Parents are the kindest audience in the world. I tell you, I've done it for fifteen years, Mr. Lawrence. There's nothing to be nervous about."

"But, Miss Foster," Mr. Lawrence asked, "do you remember how you felt the first time you gave a speech at the farewell assembly?"

"Yes, Mr. Lawrence."

"How, Miss Foster?"

"Nervous, Mr. Lawrence. Nervous."

They left before Chris had moved all the hats, and there at the bottom lay the Admiral's plumed one. Hat in hand, he straightened up, took a second to practice a flourish with the hat, then went on to take his place in the auditorium waiting for the teachers' speeches.

Miss Foster's speech was short, and friendly and comfortable. "I promise you I'll say only a few words because you have seen me and heard me so many times. Today the main speech will be given by our other sixth-grade teacher, Mr. Lawrence."

Mr. Lawrence rose and pulled nervously at the knot in his tie. Chris thought of Miss Foster and Mr. Lawrence in the hall not so very long ago.

But when Mr. Lawrence started to speak he showed no signs of nervousness. "I shall start with a quotation," he said. "The quotation that Miss Foster suggested as the theme to tie the two programs. The quotation is John Donne's famous, 'No man is an island, entire of itself, every man is a piece of the continent, a part of the main. . . .' "

Mr. Lawrence shifted his balance from one foot to the other, looked over the heads of the children, and spoke directly to the parents.

"These are the words we used as the theme to make our two programs a unit, and the theme the children can understand. Perhaps the quotation itself is still a little beyond them, and perhaps it is not.

"Let me tell you how I explained this quotation to one of these boys.

"I was walking along your wonderful beach with him one day, gazing out at the horizon. I mentioned Columbus. He immediately set up a howl because my class was having a space program and his class was going to give a play about Columbus."

Mr. Lawrence smiled. "I can still see the astonishment on his face when I told him that Columbus was a spaceman, too. This boy told me that he is going to the moon some day, and I sincerely believe him."

Chris squirmed happily in his chair.

"But perhaps he wouldn't be going if brave men long ago hadn't ventured out on an unknown sea. For one man space was out, for another space is up. Every man is influenced by what every other man does. And the long chain of history is put together link by link.

"And so I repeat, 'No man is an island, entire of itself, every man is a piece of the continent, a part of the main. . . .' And with these words, the two sixth grades will join to present the program *Spacemen All*."

Applause rang out through the auditorium. Miss Foster's class rose to go back stage to take their places. Chris' heart was beating happily. He held tightly to his plumed hat, and didn't even glance enviously at Mr. Lawrence's class all wearing space helmets.

How proud Chris was to be the early spaceman, Columbus. He knew he was playing his part well, aided by Laurie as Queen Isabella, and M.T. as King Ferdinand. But especially by Laurie.

Chris came on stage, hat in hand, and made a sweeping bow, then knelt before the King and Queen. M.T., perhaps out of nervousness, perhaps out of long custom said, "Hail, Chris." Then lamely he added, "topher."

Before the audience's titter could become a laugh, Laurie quickly ad libed. "Ah, sire," she said, putting her hand on M.T.'s arm, "be not embarrassed that you have publicly called him *Chris.*"

Then she turned to Chris. He kept his eyes downcast, for fear he would laugh if he looked at her.

"Ah, good Christopher Columbus," she went on, "while you were on your long journey, ever, ever were you in our thoughts. And oft when we talked of you in privacy, the King, my sire, spoke of you as *Chris.*"

With head up, but not daring to look at Laurie, Chris said his next line: "My King, my Queen." Then as he was supposed to, he turned and faced the audience.

Miss Foster was beaming at Laurie. Mr. Lawrence had his hand over his mouth and was shaking with suppressed laughter.

If the next line had been Chris', Laurie surely would have had to ad lib again, for then Chris saw Officer O'Looney, accompanied by Mr. Kitchenger, entering the auditorium. What were they doing there? Surely there was trouble if Mr. Kitchenger was present.

Chris allowed himself this one fleeting thought, then bent his every effort on the play. He was determined to make Mom proud of him this time.

And she seemed to be proud of him indeed. When both plays were finished and Mrs. Johnstone had given her speech, parents and children moved informally to meet one another at the back of the auditorium.

Mom rushed toward Chris. "Chris, I was so proud. I wish your dad could have been here."

That was the best praise of all.

Then Mr. Lawrence came along, grasped hold of Chris' arm and said, "Nice going, spaceman." Then he laughed. "You and Doc may have taught Laurie to climb fences, but she certainly can teach the pair of you a thing or two."

Then Chris saw Officer O'Looney and Mr. Kitchenger coming toward him. Oh, not now! Don't let anything be wrong now, just when things were all squared away. And Mr. Lawrence standing right there, too.

Officer O'Looney was friendly, but then he always was. It was Mr. Kitchenger.

"You are quite an actor, boy," the officer said. "I had no idea that was one of your accomplishments."

Chris didn't know what to say, so he just stood there.

Then Officer O'Looney said, his voice much lower this time, "Did your mother tell you I was talking to her the other day when she was hanging out the wash?"

"No, Officer O'Looney."

"I noticed that you had a pair of very interesting pajamas."

"Oh, my astronaut pajamas," Chris said in relief. They were on safe territory now.

"Very unusual buttons."

"Yes, the buttons are missile shape."

"I noticed that one was missing."

"Yes," Chris said. "Mom couldn't get one to match."

Officer O'Looney opened his hand. "Is this it?"

"Yes," Chris said eagerly. Then he closed the hand that he had just reached out toward the policeman's hand. Mr. Kitchenger's narrow eyes were taking in every movement.

Chris' heart pounded.

"Why, where did you find it, Officer O'Looney?" Mrs. Muldoon asked. "I've looked everywhere for it."

"It was found caught between the drainpipe, and the house outside Mr. Kitchenger's bathroom."

Why now? Why now, just when he had finally made Mom proud of him?"

"Christopher?" Mom's voice had an "oh no" in it, too.

"We have a theory, Mrs. Muldoon," the officer said. "We think the button became lodged there the night of the fire. We think perhaps someone climbed the drainpipe in an impulsive attempt to rescue Mr. Kitchenger, then his common sense took over and he ran to the fire box, turned in the alarm and saved Mr. Kitchenger's life."

Chris was red to the roots of his hair. Mom moved closer to him.

"Good start to the moon, Astro," Mr. Lawrence whispered. "Feet on the ground first."

"Ah, it's a man's hand you need, Chris Muldoon," Mr. Kitchenger said. And he held out his hand in friendship.